# THE UNDERCOVER CAPTAIN

RAMPANT LOON PRESS
LAKE ELMO, MINNESOTA

Published in the United States of America by Rampant Loon Press, an imprint of Rampant Loon Media LLC, P.O. Box 111, Lake Elmo, Minnesota 55042. "Rampant Loon Press" and the Rampant Loon colophon are trademarks of Rampant Loon Media LLC.

www.rampantloonmedia.com

Book design by Logotecture.

ISBN:  978-1-938834-74-5 (ebook)

ISBN: 978-1-938834-75-2 (print)

First publication: February 2017

For the Phoenix Company. They know who they are.

For the Phoenix Company. They know who they are.

# AUTHOR'S NOTE

The events in this novel take place during the nine years between the next-to-last and the last chapters of *The Counterfeit Captain*.

# THE UNDERCOVER CAPTAIN

## HENRY VOGEL

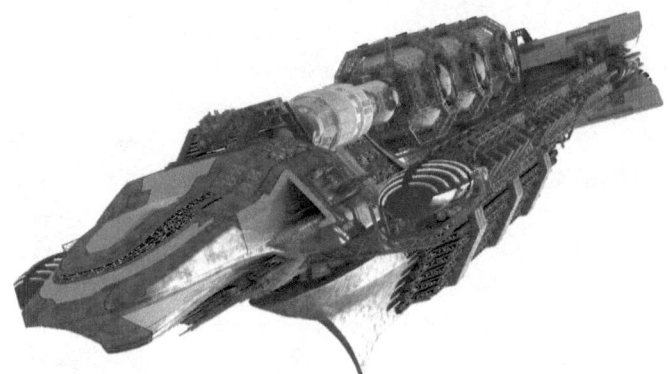

# CHAPTER ONE

*"No! You'll die if you stay in here, Sko."*

*My voice was barely audible over the wind tearing at us, rushing out into the vacuum of space. Alone, I'd have been swept along with the wind. Alone, I'd have died. But I wasn't alone. One strong arm wrapped around me, keeping me safe. The other strong arm fought from handhold to handhold, slowly pulling against the wind.*

*Sko. Brave, gentle, wise Sko. Loving, passionate, intelligent Sko. The man I was meant to spend my life with.*

*Behind us, the wind carried that bastard Smith into the squirming mass of men who formed his crew. For a brief second, the howling wind fell silent. For a brief second, Sko was free to act. Always decisive, always putting others above himself, Sko carried me to the open hatch separating the computer room from the bridge.*

*One of Smith's men popped through the knot of men and out into space. Once again, the wind roared and snatched at us. Sko put his lips against my ear so I might hear him.*

*"But you, my Captain, my love—you will live."*

*He pushed me through the hatch and slapped the emergency close button. The hatch slid shut, separating us forever. In that final second, Sko's smile said everything he did not have the time to say. In that final second, I died inside.*

The stupor I'd worked so hard to drink myself into faded with alarming rapidity. Bloody hell. This could only mean one thing, but I wasn't sober enough to remember it. It also meant the end to my three-year record of remaining falling-down drunk on the anniversary of Sko's death.

Whatever else was going on, I *was* sober enough to realize I was in a dive bar. Worse, I was sober enough to realize the bar's vid was showing one of the many versions of my story. I stared at the images through bleary eyes. A buxom blonde in a too-tight flight suit and showing lots of cleavage—something impossible to do in the real flight suits I wore—held an imploring hand toward a closed hatch.

"Lilla is the blonde, you morons. I'm a redhead."

I only realized I slurred that out loud when a couple of guys turned irritating looks my way. The bigger one of the two said, "Shut up—we're watching the vid."

The blonde with the big tits flounced to what was supposed to be a tech command console. A constipated expression crossed her face and she cried, "Your destruction is at hand, Arktu! With but the press of this ring icon, I will destroy you. With but the press of this ring icon, I will have vengeance for my beloved, my Sko!"

Ah, that constipated look was obviously meant to be an expression of triumph. Or revenge. Or something. Obviously, this actress's primary assets were still jiggling and had nothing to do with actual acting. Part of my mind wondered if she bungled the lines or if the scriptwriter was even worse at his job than the 'actress' was at hers.

The AI, in an entirely human-sounding voice, filled with entirely human emotion, cried, "No, Nancy Martin! I beg you, let me live!"

"Never!" The woman's hand rose. Her boobs bounced. She looked out of the vid at us. "This is for you, Captain Jonathan Yarrow!"

Her hand still rising, her boobs still bobbing up and down, her eyes still staring vacantly out of the vid at us, she said, "This is for you, Chief Technical Officer Deborah Armstrong!"

She struck an overly dramatic pose. "Most of all, this is for you, Sko!"

"No-o-o-o-o-o-o-o-o-o-o-o-o-o-o!" screamed the all-too-human voice as the woman's hand descended. She almost missed the console entirely, but her thumb did brush against the edge.

That's when I shot the vid unit. Blew it into a million pieces. Considering I was still sobering up, I thought it was a pretty damned good shot. None of the other patrons agreed, so I tried reasoning with them.

I adopted my most diplomatic tone of voice and sneered, "Look, you morons, that's not how it happened! And that has to be the worst-acted piece of garbage I've ever seen."

I holstered my blaster, snapped the flap over it, and flashed my most winning smile at the others in the bar. "Face it, I did you drunken idiots a favor when I shot the unit."

The drunken idiots stared at me, apparently unmoved by my impeccably reasoned and diplomatically worded pronouncement. Then the guy who told me to shut up surged up and staggered my way. A few more men followed him.

The barkeeper called, "Don't kill 'er, boys—least ways not 'till she pays for a new vid unit."

I think I held my own until the police got there. Or I would have if I hadn't gotten knocked out.

Sometime later, I woke up in a hospital room. A quick check with my implant showed I'd been out for close to two hours. I felt remarkably healthy for a woman who was on the wrong side of a one-sided bar brawl. Nothing ached. Nothing was broken. Worst of all, I was completely, depressingly sober.

A police officer stood by the door, speaking with a well-dressed, attractive woman with dark hair and dark bronze skin. The policeman wasn't pleased with what the woman said. His voice rose as he spoke, making it easy for me to hear him.

"...reckless endangerment, firing a deadly weapon in a crowded establishment, provoking a riot, destruction of private property, and whatever else I can think of to charge her with. So, no, the charges will *not* be dropped and this woman will *not* be released to you!"

A comm buzzed from the officer's pocket.

"You'd better get that, Sergeant Mooney," the woman said. "It's your chief."

Mooney grabbed his comm. His eyes widened as he read the caller ID. "Yes, Chief?"

The man listened, his expression darkening with each word. "I don't care who she is, sir. The woman is a menace and she belongs in police custody."

Mooney held the comm to his ear for another few seconds. "Yes, sir. Very clear, sir."

The officer jammed the comm into his pocket, disgust written on his face. "Maybe you got to the Chief, but that bar was pretty busted up. The owner—"

"Has already been compensated, Sergeant Mooney. In exchange, he is not pressing charges." The woman smiled without humor and patted the officer on the shoulder. "Run along now. I have private business to discuss with this woman."

Without a glance my way, Mooney stalked from the room. The woman shut the door and faced me for the first time. "Hello, Captain Martin. I'm glad you're awake."

"My correct title is Captain Martin, Retired."

The woman's expression never changed. "I'm afraid your retirement must be put on hold for a while."

"Why do I suddenly find myself wishing Sergeant Mooney was taking me into custody right now?" I asked.

"I have no idea, Captain Martin." The woman's lips turned up in an attempt at a friendly smile. "Do you mind if I call you Nancy?"

"Yes—especially since you haven't introduced yourself."

"You may call me Special Agent Erica Hampton," she said. "I work for—"

"The Federation Bureau of Investigation," I interrupted. "You do realize your agency holds no authority over me, either as a private citizen or as a Federation naval officer?"

Without a word, Hampton handed a pad to me. I scanned the orders displayed on the screen. "Why the hell have I been reactivated *and* assigned to the FBI?"

"I could tell you, Captain Martin, but—"

"Then you'd have to kill me?"

"No." The woman's tone remained level throughout this exchange, though her eyes hardened after my last interruption. "I could tell you, but you'll have to shut up long enough for me to do so."

"Fair enough," I said. "Tell me why the FBI needs me."

"We don't," Hampton said.

She reached over and tapped the pad's screen. My orders vanished, replaced by what looked like a school vid. A couple of hundred children in their mid-teens milled and posed and cut-up for the cam. The kids laughed and chatted and mostly ignored instructions called from an adult—probably a teacher—behind the cam.

"*They* most certainly do." Hampton caught my gaze and, for the first time, I saw a glimmer of humanity shining in her eyes. "Minutes after this vid was taken, those children left on an end-of-year school trip to a rim world. They never arrived."

I looked back at the vid. Unbidden, images of children slaving away in harsh conditions under Arktu's direction flooded my mind. Unbidden, I pictured the children Arktu no longer needed approaching the acid bath. Unbidden, I saw Lilla laughing with Sko.

"What do you need me to do?" I asked.

"I need you to help me find them, Captain Martin."

Without taking my eyes from the pad, I said, "Call me Nancy."

I looked up from the images cavorting on the pad and locked gazes with the other woman. "Do you think a slaver band is behind the disappearance of these kids, Special Agent Hampton?"

"That's what the Agency thinks, yes. Their destination world has two wormholes and one of them leads to the Coreward Fringes. Slavery is legal on three of the Fringe colonies and quietly tolerated on two or three more." The agent tried another smile, and this time, she got some real humanity into it. "Also, we're going to be working closely on this, so please call me Erica."

"Are you going to be my...handler? Is that the right word?"

"No, Nancy, I'm going to be your partner."

"Erica, am I going to have to drag all of this out of you one question at a time?"

"Not at all, but I'd rather save the explanations for a more secure location. I doubt anyone with slaver connections is listening in, but you're still a bit of a celebrity—especially on the anniversary of the *Ark 2's* rescue—and hospital personnel can be just as starstruck as anyone."

"Then hand me my clothes and let's get out of here."

I swung out of the bed and peeled off the hospital gown. From Erica's lack of reaction to my nudity, I guessed she had some military experience. Body self-consciousness is one of the first things you lose in boot camp.

As I pulled on my shoes, I asked, "I assume we're going to your office for this explanation?"

"No. I'm from off-planet, myself. I could get some space at the local office, but I have a more secure location in mind."

The woman paused and gave me an expectant look. Recognizing that she wanted me to ask, I sighed, "Where is that?"

"Your spaceship."

I shook my head. "I don't *have* a spaceship."

Erica grinned, showing more life in that one expression than she had during her entire visit. "You do now."

Twenty minutes later, I entered the code Erica gave me for docking bay B21 and got a look at my new ship. Make that my not-so-new ship. Scratch that, too. Make it my old ship—a Minotaur class freighter. After giving the battered hulk a quick once-over, I folded my arms and glared at my new partner.

"I'm sure this was a great ship at one time, but that time was at least fifty years before I was born. This operation of yours must have the smallest budget in Bureau history."

"You'd be surprised, Nancy. Why don't you give the *Darkheart* a closer look?"

"Seriously, *Darkheart*? How long did it take the psych geeks to come up with that?"

"Less than an hour. This is a rush job, Nancy. Every passing hour reduces our chances of finding those missing kids."

"Point taken." I headed to the rear of the ship. "Fill me in on everything while I check out my ship."

Following me, Erica said, "The FBI has been after this group for about a year. As best we can tell, the slavers are behind several other disappearances during that time. It's always a group of healthy young people—college or high school kids on school trips, mostly, though they've even taken a platoon of new military recruits on their first overnight hike."

"Let me guess, the recruits were still carrying mock weapons?" When Erica nodded, I asked, "Did they kill the drill instructors?"

"No, they're missing, too."

I got a sudden, inexplicable queasy feeling in the pit of my stomach. "Why would slavers risk taking experienced military instructors? That's just stupid."

"That bothers me, too, though I can't get the higher ups to share my concerns. They assume the recruits and their instructors will end up on a particularly rough world."

"Maybe..."

The outside of the engine compartment looked like the rest of the ship. I coded open the engine panel—they all used the default code, according to Erica—and climbed up into the engines and looked around. Things looked much different from the inside.

"Holy crap, Erica, this is the engine from a heavy cruiser!"

"Wait until you see the weapon systems."

I climbed back out, changed the panel code away from the default, and headed for the ship's hatch. Looking over my shoulder, I asked, "After working on this for a year, you've got to have some leads, right?"

"Less than you'd think. We believe one of our undercover agents got close. His last communication hinted at a possible break in the case and requested we ready a ship with specs similar to the *Darkheart*. We haven't heard from him in two weeks. Honestly, I think the case officer would still be waiting for the agent to get back in touch if the high school kids hadn't disappeared."

"This missing agent—he isn't your boyfriend or brother or something, is he?" I asked. "You're not going rogue because the Bureau is moving too slowly?"

"I met the man once in a briefing, nothing more. This is a classified operation, but it has the full backing of the Bureau."

"No offense, Erica, but I have only your word on that."

"No offense taken." She tossed her comm unit to me. "Call the local office and ask for Director Roger Preston."

The office's code was programmed into the unit, but I pulled out my pad and looked up the code. They matched, but I still punched it in by hand. In less than a minute, I had the director on the line. A minute after that, I closed the call and tossed the comm back to Erica.

"New question," I said as we entered the ship for the first time. "Why me?"

Erica hesitated for a couple of seconds and then said, "You match the profile we want for this job."

"Which is?"

"A war hero who hasn't adjusted well to life outside of the service."

"I adjusted to civilian life just fine." It was life without Sko I was having trouble with.

Erica followed me to the bridge before saying, "You're not the only person who lost a loved one in the war."

"I didn't lose a loved one in the war, Erica. I lost him in the void because of that damned AI on the *Ark 2*." I turned to face her, struggling to keep my voice from cracking, and was surprised to find her glaring at me. "What?"

She turned away. "It's nothing."

"The hell it is. Whatever is behind that glare could interfere with our teamwork at just the wrong moment. Those school children are depending on us. I am not going to let them down because we couldn't be upfront and open with each other." I found myself glaring back at Erica. Consciously toning down my gaze, I said, "So spill it. I'm a big girl. I can handle whatever you have to say."

"Okay." Erica took a moment, obviously composing herself, before asking, "What makes you so special? Why are you still wallowing in your misery and why do I have to tread so damned lightly around you because of it?"

"Excuse me?"

"You heard me. I did my grieving and then got on with my life—just like everyone else who fought in the war. It wasn't easy. It still isn't easy. But I did it. The great Nancy Martin, though, spends years grieving over her lost love, crawling into and out of the bottle as she sees fit." Erica's glare returned. "Why can't you find a way to move on with your life?"

"Who did you lose?"

"My husband. He was killed in the Battle of Cath."

I winced. That battle was fought three days after I reset the *Ark 2's* AI, two days after the ceasefire, and one day *before* the fastest messenger drone could reach the Cath System. "That must have been especially painful for you, Erica. Your husband was assigned to the Second Battle Group?"

Erica shook her head. "We were both part of the Triple F."

I searched my memory for that nickname and came up empty. "I'm sorry but I don't recognize that unit."

Erica caught and held my eyes in her challenging gaze. "It's official designation was the Fourth Fringe Fleet."

"Oh." I couldn't think of anything else to say to her revelation. "How long had you been married?"

"Sixteen days."

"I am so sorry, Erica."

Blinking her eyes rapidly, she turned away from me. I waited for her to regain her composure, not speaking again until she turned back to me.

"After you lost your husband, can I assume all your friends, family, and shipmates went out of their way to express their sympathy?" Erica nodded, so I continued, "Did you both appreciate the thoughts behind their condolences and wish they'd kept silent?"

Erica's eyes widened slightly. "Yes! Just when my mind stopped whirling and settled on something other than Gerard's death, someone would tell me how sorry they were. All my pain and sorrow came rushing back again, but I had to smile and thank them for being so kind. At the time, it felt like I was thanking them for ripping away newly formed scab."

"How long did it take people to stop doing that?"

"I don't know. Two weeks, maybe? There was still the odd friend or relative who hadn't seen me who would bring it up, but those were so far between that I'd had time to do the worst of my grieving."

"In the three years since Sko's death, I've never gone more than eight waking and sober hours without someone ripping the scab off of my wound."

"Oh my God!"

I shrugged. "There are thousands of news stories, books, and vids about the *Ark 2*. Every single one of them says something about Sko and me. And when anyone who's ever read or watched one of them recognizes me or is introduced to me, the very first thing they say is 'I'm so very sorry about Sko.' I smile and thank them for their kind words because they think they're just being sympathetic. But, inside, I'm screaming because their words have brought back the same anguish I felt when I first discovered Sko was gone."

"I never realized, Nancy. And now I've just ripped your scab off again. I'm sorry." Erica enveloped me in a hug. After a few seconds, she said, "You know, at first, I blamed you for Gerard's death. If only you had reset that damned AI a day sooner, he wouldn't have died. If only you hadn't wasted time chasing all around the ship and just gone straight for the captain's cabin, you could have done it. Then my life wouldn't have been ripped apart in a useless battle fought after a useless war ended. If only... Eventually, after I worked through the worst of my grief, I came to my senses."

We released each other and wiped at our eyes. Desperate to talk about anything but Sko, I took the discussion off on a tangent.

"If you fought for the Fringers, how did you end up in the FBI?"

Erica gave me a humorless smile. "When the war ended, my home planet up and joined the Federation. Tens of thousands of us fought and a lot of them died so we could be free of Federation influence, and when it was over, the politicians screwed us. When the FBI recruited me, I said 'what the hell' and signed on."

"So you fit the same profile I do."

"Yep. I'm the bitter veteran who lost her husband fighting for a lost cause."

"And we're two bitter women tolerating each other as, what? Penance for our sins or something?"

"Something like that. The point, Nancy, is we're exactly the kind of people criminals look for. Life screwed us so they assume we're looking to screw life back. Did I mention you're a dozen payments behind on the ship? That's almost like an engraved invitation into the underbelly of civilization."

"And the ship's name? The profilers chose *Darkheart* for both of us, didn't they?"

Erica nodded as I settled into the pilot's seat and checked the readouts. Everything looked good. We even had a full tank of reaction mass.

"Have we got provisions for the trip?" I asked. "For that matter, where are we going?"

"Osnade. It's just outside the Federation border. That's where the agent disappeared. We've got plenty of provisions for the trip."

I flashed a feral grin at Erica. "Then let's go rescue kids and kick slaver ass!"

"We can't leave, yet, Nancy," Erica said. "We're still waiting for our cargo."

"We've got cargo?" I asked.

"It's all part of our cover. We have a contract for a load of chemicals scheduled for rush delivery. Only, when we get to Osnade we'll discover our contractor is bankrupt and can't pay us."

I nodded in understanding. "If our goal is to look desperate, I'll need to dump reaction mass during our approach to Osnade. Nothing says desperation like a ship's captain who doesn't have the money to lift off again."

"Nice touch, Nancy," Erica said. "No one involved in planning the operation thought of that."

"My parents ran a small freighter while I was growing up. They never ended up as deeply underwater as we want to appear, but they came close more than once." Memories of my childhood rushed in, triggering another thought. "These chemicals we're waiting for—can they be used to make illegal drugs?"

"Yes. We're carrying all the most difficult to obtain ingredients for top-grade Dreamweaver." Erica studied my expression carefully. "Is that going to be a problem?"

"Considering the stakes, no," I mused, "but simple desperation shouldn't be enough to make us sell to drug dealers. We should have no other choice. Otherwise, we'll look too eager and scare off our prey."

"Is that based on personal experience?"

I shook my head. "Personal observation. Dad pointed out more than one free trader who was slowly buckling under the weight of debt and desperation. I'm sure they all vowed to break the law just one time, to go straight again once they paid off everyone they owed. Crossing that line is hard the first time, but the second time isn't nearly as hard, and the third time is almost easy."

"I see your point, but other than making sure we're not too easy to coax to the wrong side of the law, I don't see what it has to do with this operation."

"Liquor is the lubricant that makes it all work. I never knew a captain who went bad without first crawling into a bottle. None of them were entirely sober when they took their first illegal job and most of them were never entirely sober again." I rubbed my temples. "I'm halfway into that bottle already, but I can't help those kids if I'm drunk."

"So, you want *me* to be the drunk? I don't—"

"No, Erica, I've earned that role and have got to keep it up. But I think we should permanently enable my implant's alcohol scrubber so I can drink and *pretend* I'm drunk."

The scrubber isn't classified by the military, but no serving member ever tells civilians about it. Since the scrubber keeps active duty personnel from getting anything more than slightly tipsy, we can always win drinking bets with civilians. The filter is turned off as part of mustering out, which is why I could drink myself into a stupor instead of dealing with Sko's death. The filter cleared my haze earlier in the day and led to the big bar fight. And the fight fit perfectly with the cover story the FBI wanted for me. Continued drinking fit the story, too, but I couldn't help those kids if I was facedown in a puddle of my own drool.

"We're way ahead of you, Nancy. No one turned off the filter after your fight in the bar."

I bristled at the assumptions behind that decision. "What if I'd turned you down? Did you ever think of that?"

"Not much," Erica replied. "Everyone who read your file knew you'd accept the mission. You've got a protective streak at least two klicks wide."

"What makes you think the criminals won't know that, too?"

"They don't have access to your file. It's got details never found in any of the vids about the *Ark 2* or in any of the books written about it. You've also got to remember that a lot of crooks assume hero stories are mostly made up and spoon-fed to a gullible public. They *want* to believe there's less to you than the stories say. It makes them feel better about their own choices—well, the ones with some kind of conscience, anyway."

Before we could debate this any further, the cargo we were waiting for showed up. We spent the rest of the day getting it properly stowed. With all of the official forms stored on our pads, we filed our flight plan for Osnade. Forty-three minutes later, I piloted the *Darkheart* out of the atmosphere and set course for the first wormhole in our journey.

"I thought the ship would be faster than this," Erica said, watching our speed climb slowly.

"It is," I said, "but this pace is the best *Darkheart* could make with her original engine. I doubt anyone is watching, but I'm not willing to gamble our lives and the lives of those kids on it."

"Smart. Have I mentioned that you're a natural at this, Nancy?"

"No, and don't mention it again until those kids are safe."

"Until?" Erica flashed a smile at me. "I like the way you think, Nancy."

On that positive note, our ship entered the wormhole.

# CHAPTER TWO

One week later, it looked like Erica's plan was working quite well. Since we landed, I'd visited a lot of businesses, ostensibly looking for a buyer for my cargo. I'll hand it to the planners at the FBI—they picked chemicals we could never move on Osnade. Business number twenty-seven was no different than the previous twenty-six.

"Look, I wish I could help you, but I only use a couple of kilos of that stuff every year."

I believed the man sitting on the other side of the desk. He had an earnest and honest air about him, as well as a good reputation in Praka, the largest city on the rim world of Osnade. I stood, stretching my hand across the desk to shake his.

"I understand. Thank you for taking the time to meet with me, Mr. Tawiah."

"I'm just sorry you find yourself in such a terrible situation, Captain Martin," Tawiah said.

"The life of a free trader is more difficult than my partner and I originally imagined," I said, playing my role as the vet who blew her pension on a pipe dream to the hilt.

"I'm sure things will turn around for you soon, Captain."

The man's eyes, however, said he'd witnessed this scene several times in the past and wondered why so many people assumed running a business was easy. It's a good question, one that irritated my father no end. When Dad found himself barely treading water, people with no business experience happily told him everything they thought he was doing wrong. When, after careful observation and monitoring of trends, Dad made a big score, those same people readily dismissed his success as simple luck. Somehow, I thought Tawiah and Dad could easily spend all day swapping such stories.

Back on the street, I set off toward our new docking bay—the much cheaper one we'd moved the *Darkheart* to once we 'discovered' our client was bankrupt. The walk was long and the route led right to the poorer part of Praka. The crew members from most of the ships docked near us took taxis right to their docking bays—it's safer that way. Then again, most crew members don't own a blaster, much less wear it on their hip.

Even openly carried pistols didn't stop one little gang of five guys from trying to mug us. Erica and I had the poor grace to attack as soon as the first blade appeared. We stunned two of them, broke another one's elbow, and let the other two run off with nothing more than a few insults hurled at their backs. Word got around quickly enough and no one else bothered us. I had some hope our fight would act as a bit of an audition for the kinds of people we wanted to find, but four days had passed without anyone approaching us.

I followed my standard protocol and stopped at the Red Dog, a dive bar near our docking bay with a less than licit reputation among free traders. I trudged up to Max, the bartender, with my head down and my hands stuffed in the pockets of my flight jacket. In a galaxy brimming with automated systems, every bar worth visiting has a human running the place. An AI just can't read moods like a human, much less lend a sympathetic ear or be a source of useful information.

"Hey, Max. Whiskey. Double. That cheap crap you always give me," I said, keeping my head down.

"How 'bout some o' the good stuff, Nance?" Max asked.

I flat out hate it when people call me 'Nance'. Nancy is two freaking syllables. *Two.* We're not talking about a hard name to pronounce, much less a long one. But there's always someone who decides to go for the nickname, to be more familiar with me than they have earned. Usually, I'd smack someone like Max down hard for going there. But I might need Max to make that first illicit contact, so I let him get away with it.

"You know I can't afford the good stuff," I said. "Not if I want to eat today."

"Already paid for." Max put a glass and an entire bottle of really good stuff—the label said it was imported all the way from Tennessee, back on Earth—and pointed to a back corner booth. A woman sat there, her attention focused entirely on her pocket pad.

"You think she wants to buy my cargo, Max?"

Max shrugged. "Ask her."

I scooped up the glass and the bottle. "I will."

The woman didn't look up as I slid into the booth. She paid no attention as I poured a double shot of whiskey and knocked it back. I gave a real sigh of contentment. I'd guzzled so much cheap crap over the last few days that I'd almost forgotten what good whiskey tasted like. Without hesitation, I poured another shot. This time, I swirled the whiskey around in my mouth before swallowing. Once again, I sighed.

"Are you going to offer me some whiskey?" the woman asked, never once looking up from her pad.

"Nope," I said, carefully pouring another shot. "I might give you some if you ask."

"I paid for the bottle." The woman's voice remained level, almost monotone.

"And then gave it to me."

"An excellent point, Captain Martin. As it happens, I don't like whiskey."

"That's your problem."

"And problem is a cargo you can't sell, dwindling funds, and a ship too low on reaction mass to lift off."

I lifted my glass as if in a toast to the woman. "Thus, the whiskey."

The woman brought her head up. Her gray eyes caught my blue ones and held them. "Most captains in your situation would have already offered to sell their cargo to me."

"I'm not most captains." The woman kept staring into my eyes, so I elaborated. Tapping the bottle, I said, "You paid for this. You waited here for me. You want something from me. I'm content to drink until you get around telling me what it is."

The woman's perfectly shaped eyebrows rose. "You are not what I expected, Captain Martin."

"I took on an ill-advised cargo and made the mistake of running my ship too close to the edge," I said. "That doesn't mean I'm stupid."

"Quite." The woman put down her pad and gave me her full attention for the first time. "Tell me about your ship's engine."

After she asked the question, I realized it shouldn't surprise me. A smuggler in a tight spot has a limited number of options and the best one is almost always running. A smuggler whose ship can't run will have a very short career. Knowing that, just how much of the truth should I tell this woman? And how much did she already know?

"The *Darkheart* is equipped with the engine from a heavy cruiser. She'll be plenty fast enough for anything you want her to do."

The woman's mouth crooked up in a slight smile. "I imagine you wouldn't be in your current situation if you hadn't wasted so much money buying more engine than you need."

"My ship has more engine than she has *needed* so far. That doesn't mean she won't need it someday." If the woman knew anything about Federation laws—and I felt certain she did—she knew private citizens couldn't legally own military engines. She would also know they were prohibitively expensive on the black market. "Who says I wasted any money on the engine?"

"Do tell, Captain."

"Let's just say I have friends throughout the navy. Some of them...found...the engine for me."

"Those are some good friends to have. Did they also... find...your ship's weapons systems?"

Now I realized why it took so long for this first contact to take place. The woman was checking up on us, including breaking into our docking bay and examining our ship. That's a positive development. I think.

"My partner armed the ship. You want me to call her and have her drop by?"

The woman checked the time on her pad. "No need. She should be here in the next ten to fifteen minutes."

"You've been watching us."

"People I represent have, yes."

"Do you like what you've seen so far?"

"We wouldn't be having this conversation if we didn't, Captain Martin."

"Do you have a name?"

"You may call me Miss Perkins."

"That's a rather old fashioned form of address, Miss Perkins."

Her lips curved up in a slight smile again. "We like old fashioned ways on Osnade, Captain Martin."

Miss Perkins and I watched each other for the next twelve minutes, with me breaking off the staring match twice to down shots of whiskey. When Erica finally got to the bar, I told her to grab a glass and join us. Our hostess told me to keep quiet and asked Erica the same series of questions she asked me. The hours we spent fleshing out our cover stories during the trip to Osnade paid off as Erica gave essentially the same story I did.

Miss Perkins considered us for a minute after she finished questioning Erica. In the end, she smiled broadly at us both. "Ladies, I believe we can do business."

Erica and I exchanged glances, then she said, "Does that mean you want to buy our cargo?"

"No, but I will take it off your hands and dispose of it myself. In return, you'll transport a cargo for me and I'll fully fuel and provision your ship."

"How much do we get paid for the delivery?"

"Considering your dire straights, the reaction mass and provisions should be more than enough for you."

"In other words," I said, "we don't get paid at all."

"Not in cash, but if this goes well, you will be well paid for your next delivery."

I nodded slowly. "What, exactly, are we delivering?"

"Supplies."

"That's rather non-specific," Erica said.

"Do you have a problem with that?" Miss Perkins asked.

Erica and I exchanged a quick look and then shook our heads.

Miss Perkins smiled thinly. "Excellent. I'll set everything in motion. You leave tomorrow morning."

I looked at Erica. When she shrugged, I said, "Yeah, okay."

Miss Perkins stood. "I'll have a crew at your docking bay in one hour to unload your unclaimed cargo. The crew will load my departing cargo once your hold is clear."

Erica and I scooted out of the booth. I kept a hand wrapped around the neck of the whiskey bottle. I swung it around a bit, just in case Miss Perkins hadn't noticed.

"What kind of equipment will we need to load and unload your cargo?" Erica asked.

"None. My crew will bring everything they need."

"That's great here on Osnade," Erica said, "but what do we do when delivering the cargo?"

"My crew will bring everything they need for loading and unloading of the cargo," Miss Perkins said.

"Your men are coming with us?" I asked as if this thought never crossed my mind. Of course, it actually made perfect sense for Miss Perkins to maintain complete control over our first cargo.

"My *crew* is composed of men and women, Captain Martin," Miss Perkins said, her tone prim.

"Whatever." I swung the bottle in an erratic arc meant to encompass most of the planet. "I was just trying to be like one of you old fashioned Osnadians. *Miss* Perkins."

"Very amusing, Captain Martin. If all goes well on this delivery run and you find yourself staying on, I advise procuring an Osnadian guidebook. You have much to learn about our ways." Miss Perkins flashed a perfunctory smile. "Thank you, ladies. I'll see you you shortly."

The woman swept away in a swirl of skirts. Damned if one of the rough-looking drunks near the door didn't jump up and open the door for her, too. She nodded politely to the man, who bobbed his head in return. He released the door and went back to his seat, completely ignoring Erica and me.

Out on the street, I quietly asked, "Do you think the guy reacted to the skirt or Miss Perkins' reputation among the Osnadian underclass?"

"What makes you think she isn't a reputable businesswoman?" Erica asked.

"Uh, everything?" I replied.

"Such as?"

"Her smug certainty we would accept the offer. Her knowledge of the *Darkheart's* capabilities. Her secrecy. Her insistence on total control over the cargo. Her appearance, which is completely out of place in this part of town. Her willingness to walk these streets alone after dark." I looked at my companion. "What makes you think she is a reputable businesswoman?"

"Absolutely nothing," Erica replied. "I wanted to see how observant you were."

"Did I pass?"

"Yes." She flagged down a passing taxi. "Get in. I want to run some system checks before Miss Perkins' crew arrives."

The next hour passed quickly as Erica and I checked the concealed cams built into the *Darkheart* by the FBI. She wasn't fully satisfied with our rushed testing, but time was running out.

"You know we tested these systems every day during our trip to Osnade," I said. "They should work just fine."

"Nancy, when you were flying missions for the Fed Navy, what would you have said to a mechanic who insisted he'd checked your fighter's weapons the day before?"

"Nothing fit for polite company," I admitted, "though I don't think comparing a state-of-the-art warship with a collection of off-the-shelf cams is—"

"These aren't your average cams," Erica said. "They are virtually undetectable while recording extremely highly detailed vids and picking up the slightest sounds—even ones the human ear can't detect."

I held my hands up in mock surrender. "Okay. I promise I won't make ill-advised comments about equipment I know nothing about. Fair enough?"

"Yep." Erica carefully slid the vid controls, which were under the pilot's console, shut. She ran her thumb over the tiny seam and it sealed itself, leaving the appearance of a single sheet of metal. Just as she stood up, our comm buzzed.

"This is the *Darkheart*," I said into the comm, "Captain Martin speaking."

"My crew is here to unload your ship," Miss Perkins said.

"I'll come down and let you in."

A couple of minutes later, Miss Perkins and I stood to one side as her crew of ten—seven men and three women—began unloading our 'unclaimed' cargo. They were fast and efficient, maneuvering float pallets with practiced ease. In far less time than I'd believed possible, our cargo hold was empty and Miss Perkins' driver guided his truck out of the docking bay and out of sight. The other truck must have been waiting outside because its driver backed into the docking bay as soon as the way was clear.

"I'll have to supervise the loading and securing of the cargo," I said.

"You most certainly will not," Miss Perkins said. "My crew is entirely capable of handling this."

"Your crew won't be piloting this ship." I pointed to the first of many cubical crates, each three meters on a side. "Even if those crates weigh exactly the same, I must make sure the balance is just right."

"My crew foreman has twenty years of experience, Captain Martin. I trust him implicitly."

"Are you coming with us on this trip, Miss Perkins?"

"Goodness, no."

"Then you will let me supervise this or you can find another ship."

Miss Perkins and I glared at each other for about ten seconds before she called, "Sam, please come over here."

A broad-shouldered man at least fifteen years older than me approached and doffed his cap. "Yes, ma'am?"

"How many times have you supervised the loading of a Minotaur class freighter, Sam?" she asked.

The man barked a short laugh. "More times than I can count, ma'am."

Miss Perkins turned her glare back at me. "There, Captain. My foreman is more than capable of handling this."

I toned down my glare as I swung my eyes from the woman to her foreman. "Sam, how many times have you supervised the loading of a Minotaur class freighter equipped with a Nexus class engine? Or, for that matter, *any* ship with that engine?"

Sam fidgeted with his hat for a moment, as if not wanting to answer the question. Finally, he said, "None, Captain Martin."

"Will *you* be riding on the ship, Sam?" I asked.

"Yes, Captain. Me and the crew are coming along to take care of the cargo at all stops."

"What do you think will happen if we are forced to make a full power burn and the cargo is even slightly out of balance?" I pressed.

"I...don't know, Captain."

"Do you want to find out?"

Sam shook his head. "No, Captain."

I turned back to Miss Perkins and whipped up my best displeased-officer glare. "Satisfied?"

Miss Perkins gave a slight nod. "You have made your point quite admirably, Captain. You may supervise the loading and distribution of the cargo in your hold. You may *not* open any of the crates."

"Lady, I couldn't care less what's in those crates," I lied, "but I'll have to record the weight of each crate. We may have to rebalance each time we offload some of these crates."

Miss Perkins flashed a sour smile and said, "I understand, Captain Martin."

Maybe she really did understand or maybe she was just willing to accept Sam's word, but I learned a couple of things from the exchange. First, Miss Perkins did not like being crossed, even when she was in the wrong. Maybe especially when she was in the wrong. She compressed her lips into a thin line as the foreman and I turned toward the cargo hold.

Second, neither Sam nor Miss Perkins was a pilot. If they were, they wouldn't have accepted my explanation quite so readily. It's not that I lied—proper ship balance is important when you're working with high-powered engines—but every pilot in the navy learns how to handle out-of-balance ships. You never know when large pieces of your ship will get blown off in combat, forcing the pilot to manually compensate for the imbalance. Of course, I really do prefer flying a properly trimmed ship.

Loading took much longer than unloading, further increasing Miss Perkins' quiet displeasure. I added a lack of patience to my list of her virtues. I worked her crew for six hours before declaring myself satisfied with the ship's balance. In truth, I spent the last two hours just moving stuff around for the hell of it and watching Miss Perkins' lips grow thinner and thinner.

"That's got it, Miss Perkins," I said, my tone jovial. "Thank you for your patience."

I got a short nod in return. Then the woman handed me a portable pad. "Your itinerary, Captain Martin."

I scrolled through the various planets and the route Miss Perkins laid out for us. "This is a very inefficient route, Miss Perkins. You've got us going to Tokra first, but there are three closer planets. Would you like me to—"

"No, Captain Martin, I would *not* like you to do anything except follow the route. *Exactly* as laid out, with *no* deviations. Is that perfectly clear?"

I shrugged. "You're the boss and you're covering our expenses."

"Indeed, I am." Miss Perkins checked her chrono. "I believe it's time for you to lift off, Captain."

I raised an eyebrow. "I thought you said we would leave tomorrow morning."

The woman tapped her chrono and it projected a holo of the time between us. It was shortly past midnight. "It *is* morning, Captain."

"So it is, Miss Perkins." I gave her a slight bow and a mocking salute. "If you'll excuse me?"

Without waiting for an acknowledgment, I headed for the pilot's compartment. Thirty-six minutes later, the *Darkheart* rose gracefully through the black skies of Osnade and into space.

Minotaur freighters are designed for a crew of five and we had twelve people on board. To make matters worse, Erica and I refused the freight handlers' demand that the two of us share a single cabin. The complaints began before we took off. I handled them succinctly.

"My ship, my rules."

The crew immediately appealed to Sam. The first man to bitch about the arrangement asked, "Are you gonna let her get away with that?"

Sam looked over at Erica and me, both of us with our arms crossed and leaning nonchalantly against opposite bulkheads. I expect the pair of us looked pretty hot, with Erica's bronze complexion and flowing black hair contrasting sharply with my pale skin and red ponytail. Add in skintight flight suits and blaster holsters riding low on our right hips and I thought we were the perfect teenage-boy-fantasy flight crew.

We both gave Sam our best no-nonsense stares. He already had my measure from the discussion with Miss Perkins. Now he got Erica's measure.

"Her ship. Her rules." Voices rose in protest after Sam spoke, so he added, "If you don't like it, get off now and tell Miss Perkins you don't want to go."

That shut them up in a heartbeat. Was Miss Perkins *that* frightening or did she just have frightening friends? It was an important question, one we'd need to answer eventually, but for now, her reputation served my purposes.

Just because they stopped complaining about sleeping arrangements didn't mean they stopped complaining. They left us alone during the takeoff, mostly because everyone was strapped in, but once we reached space it didn't take long for the crew to get bored.

One of the women was the first to wander into the pilot's compartment. "What kind of entertainment have you got on this bucket?"

"You're not allowed in this compartment," I said.

"The hatch was open," the woman said

"So what?"

"That's like an invitation."

"No, it's so Erica or I can get aft quickly in case something goes wrong."

"Hey, nobody said nothing 'bout ship problems." The woman's eyes widened in alarm. "What's wrong?"

"Nothing is wrong," I sighed.

"But you said—"

"I said *in case*. Now, please get out of the pilot's compartment and tell the others they aren't allowed up here, either."

"But what about entertainment?"

"Didn't you bring anything with you?" Erica asked. "Books or vids on your pads, maybe?"

"Books? Get real, sister. And I seen all my vids. I want something different."

"Once we're clear of the traffic around Osnade, I'll see what I can find for you," I said.

"How long will that take?"

"A couple of hours. Longer if you stand there distracting me."

"That's a long—"

I spun away from the controls and glared at the woman. "Get. Out."

"Okay, I'm going. Geez." Holding her hands up in mock defense, the woman backed out of the compartment. Erica got up and slid the hatch shut. Just before it closed, the woman called, "What about if something goes wrong and you can't get to it in time?"

"Then we'll all die and it will be your fault," Erica hissed just before the hatch closed.

"Thank you, Erica," I said, laughing. "I needed that."

"It's obvious our employer didn't hire these people for their brains," Erica said, shaking her head in disgust.

"Don't underestimate Sam. He plays the part of the big, dumb lug, but I think he's a lot smarter than he lets on."

"I agree. His eyes are always moving and I doubt much happens he isn't aware of." Erica looked over at me as I reclined in my seat and ignored the ship's controls. "Shouldn't you be piloting through the traffic close to the planet?"

I waved a hand in dismissal. "Pffft. The autopilot can handle this easily. I'm close enough to jump in if something comes up, of course. I just played up the traffic to get rid of that irritating woman." Lowering my voice to a whisper, I asked, "Have you scanned the compartment for listening devices?"

Erica lowered her voice to match mine. "We're clear, but keep whispering. No sense in taking chances."

I nodded. "What are the odds that Miss Perkins is connected to the people we want?"

"Surprisingly good. In our missing agent's last report, he said the people he was watching needed unobtrusive transports like this one. We had a shipyard working around the clock to put the *Darkheart* together."

I jerked a thumb over my shoulder and toward the rest of the ship. "They could pack five stasis units inside those big crates—and that's for the top-of-the-line military grade ones. If the slavers were willing to cut corners and take a few risks, they could pack as many as nine in each crate. We could be carrying more than two hundred people back there and never know it."

"We'll know exactly what's in those crates once I go back there and look inside some of them," Erica said.

"What are you going to do, waltz right past ten people and through the airlock into the hold without any of them noticing?"

"I'm trained for this sort of thing, Nancy. All we have to do is get them embroiled in some vid and I can handle the rest."

"If most of them are like our recent visitor, you're probably right. But do you remember what we both said about Sam?"

"Don't worry about it," she insisted. "Why don't you go find that vid unit you promised the woman?"

I laced my hands behind my head and leaned even farther back. "It hasn't been two hours, yet."

Erica and I took turns napping while we waited for my time limit to pass. We gave it an extra twenty minutes just because we could. I emerged from the pilot's compartment to find six of Sam's crew waiting just outside the door.

"Took you long enough," one of the men muttered.

I glared at the man and he backed up a step. "Gee, I'm sorry paying attention to my duties got in the way of your fun. I foolishly thought you'd rather not crash into another ship out here. Next time, I'll remember you value vids more than your life."

The man's face hardened, but the woman who bothered us first stepped in front of him. "Lloyd didn't mean nothing, Captain. *Right*, Lloyd?"

A couple of seconds passed before Lloyd ground out, "Right, Wanda."

I spent the next fifteen minutes wandering around the crew area, pretending to look for the vid player. I knew exactly where it was, but felt like playing with Lloyd's mind a bit. What can I say? Simple things amuse me.

Cries of relief came from all around when I 'found' the player. I hooked it up in the common area and brought up the catalog. The crew was arguing over vids before I even left the compartment.

Nearly an hour later, long after the vid arguments were over, Erica slipped quietly out of our compartment. I'll grant that she knows her stuff. We were in the middle of a conversation when she left. I looked away for a second or two and, when I looked back, she was gone. As a precaution, I finished what I had to say and settled down to wait for her.

Thirty minutes later, Erica returned, closed the hatch, and slumped into her seat. "You were right. I never heard Sam move, but he just appeared next to me at the airlock into the docking bay."

"What did you tell him?"

"Standard stuff about making sure the cargo didn't shift during takeoff. Then I invited him to help me inspect the cargo. We each grabbed an atmosphere harness and did just that." Erica flashed a humorless smile. "On the plus side, the cargo is nice and secure."

"On the minus side," I said, "we still don't know what's in the crates."

"Exactly," my partner agreed. "And this will be a wasted trip if we don't get a peek."

"Oh, don't worry, Erica," I said, "I can get back there without Sam seeing me go."

"How? Can you turn invisible or something?"

"No, I'll just take a route he won't expect." I looked at Erica.

"Let me guess. You're going to go outside?" At my nod, Erica shook her head. "I already thought of that. All it takes is one of them wandering up here while you're gone and we're busted."

"Don't worry, I've got that covered," I said. "You're going to love it, too."

Strangely enough, she hated it.

"It's standard procedure," I said, raising my voice over the now-standard sound of the freight crew's complaints.

A man the others called Nate stepped in front of me, arms crossed. "I ain't never spent no wormhole jump belted to my seat so's no pilot can take tests."

I took a couple of seconds to parse through the man's triple negative with the added-in single negative. That made it tricky, but I was confident he couldn't follow my grammarian logic if his life depended on it. I smiled brightly into his glare and said, "That's good. It means you're used to this and can explain the importance of it to everyone else."

"What kind of crazy talk is that, woman?" Nate demanded, his face reddening.

"First, you will call me Captain. Is that clear?" I glared up at the man until he gave a short nod. "Second, you just said you never went through a wormhole where the pilot didn't perform system tests."

"That ain't what I said!"

"Shut up, Nate," Sam said, pushing in front of his crew. "Captain, please explain this situation to me using the least technical words you can."

"Our safety systems detected a...I guess 'shimmy' is as good a word as any...in the aft inertial dampeners when we entered the wormhole." I gave a vague wave toward the pilot's cabin. "I'll be happy to show you the readings if you want."

Sam motioned me to lead the way, saying, "And what does the shimmy mean."

"Probably nothing," I said, "but it could be the first indicator that the dampeners are failing."

*That* shut down the muttering from the crew. Anyone who has ever traveled through a wormhole hears stories about inertial dampener failure. There are stories of entire crews blasted to atoms when their ship went translight in a fraction of a second. The worst stories are of partial failures, where part of the crew is left perfectly healthy while their friends, sometimes their families, disintegrate in a haze of red mist.

Sam followed me to the controls and watched as I brought up the tolerance readings for the aft inertial dampeners. Pointing at one row of numbers, I said, "This series of readings is off by point two percent. We can realign the dampeners, but need the tests to make sure the new alignment is holding."

The readings were off by that much, too. The FBI's ship design team didn't miss a trick. Falsifying system checks is so vital to certain undercover missions—ones like ours—that agents can edit those readings directly, modifying them to create the appearance of whatever disaster fits the agent's needs.

I didn't even know about it until I told Erica I was just going to assume Sam and the others wouldn't know a proper alignment reading if it bit them in the ass. Somewhat hesitantly Erica told me she could edit the readings. I guess she was afraid I'd get pissed off that she'd kept the information from me. She looked relieved when I waved it off and told her what to edit.

Sam leaned over me and peered at the number. "How much of the ship is covered by the aft dampeners?"

"Everything on the other side of that hatch," I replied, pointing at the entrance to the pilot's compartment. "Controls are labeled for pilots, Sam. Everything behind my compartment is aft to me."

"Huh." Sam stood up. "What if you just want to fix the shimmy? Can you do that without tests?"

"We can route the systems around the problem, but that makes for more expensive repairs." Mentally holding my breath, I added, "Give the word and I'll do that. Your people won't have to be strapped in but you'll have to cover my repair costs."

"And why do we have to strap in?"

"Because we have to stress the systems a bit, which means making some quick attitude changes. If you're not strapped in, you could get thrown around and injured."

"I didn't think you could do that sort of stuff inside a wormhole."

"Well, we can. We just don't do it unless it's important," I said. "Like now."

"All right. We'll get strapped in. How long will this take?"

"An hour, give or take a bit. I'll give you five minutes to strap in." As Sam walked out, I called after him, "This is a short wormhole transit, Sam. We've got about an hour and fifteen minutes left. Tell your people to stay put and leave us alone."

As soon as the hatch slid shut, Erica whispered, "Are you sure this is such a good idea? Can't we—"

"There isn't any other emergency we can concoct which will keep the crew in place long enough for me to do this." I strapped on an EVA harness while I talked. "And yes, Erica, I have to be the one to do it. I'm the only one of us with EVA experience."

"Have you ever gone outside while your ship was inside a wormhole?"

"No, but it *has* been done." When Erica opened her mouth to speak, I overrode her. "Yes, most of them came back."

"Most? All the more reason I—"

"Erica, you can land this ship almost as well as I can if anything happens to me. You told me that's why they picked you for this assignment. What you can't do nearly as well is safely move down the outside of the ship and into the freight compartment. Now, stop complaining and double-check my harness for me."

She didn't stop complaining, but Erica did give me a thumbs-up for the harness. "What should I do if one of the crew bangs on the door and asks to speak to you?"

"As long as I'm in the cargo hold, you can patch my comm into the intercom. If I'm in transit one way or the other, you'll just have to temporize until I can talk."

"I still don't understand why comms don't work outside of the ship, Nancy."

"Neither do I, though the smart science people all assure me it makes perfect sense."

"And what if something happens to you out there? Like you lose your grip or something?"

I met Erica's gaze with my own level stare. "Then I will die and you'll have to finish the mission alone."

To my surprise, Erica gave me a quick hug. "Then don't lose your grip."

"I'll do my best not to," I replied, returning her squeeze.

I stepped into the emergency airlock. "You've cut the alarms on the airlocks?"

"Of course."

With a nod, I cycled the airlock and carefully pulled myself out of the *Darkheart* and into the wormhole.

I've gone outside of a ship plenty of times. Everyone in the navy gets extensive EVA training but engineers and fighter pilots get even more. Engineers never know when they'll have to go out and fix something. Fighter pilots may have to fix their ship, though swapping out parts is about the best we can manage, or just get out of a dying spacecraft. In other words, people who can't handle staring into the black of space never make it as pilots. Never.

The inside of a wormhole isn't like normal space. Not at all. It's like something out of a gothic horror vid. Mist swirls all around you, driven by unseen and unfelt winds, restricting your range of vision to a few meters. The comm, normally filled with no-nonsense chatter in normal space—even when a pilot is abandoning her ship—is eerily silent. But the silence vanishes within the first few seconds, replaced by unintelligible whispers that work on your nerves with each passing minute. Those whispers have sent strong men with hundreds of hours of EVA experience fleeing back to the safety of their ship quivering in fear.

I wanted to retreat and do some fearful quivering, too, but that just wasn't an option. Someone had to find out what was inside those containers and I was the logical person to do it. When the whispers began, I tried humming the navy anthem. It didn't drown out the insidious voices, but it did give me something else to listen to. Gritting my teeth, I clipped my first safety line to the ring just outside of the airlock and pulled myself down the outer skin of the *Darkheart*. A meter later, I clipped my second line and then released the first one. It's slow going, moving from one ring to the next, clipping and unclipping safety lines, but when certain death is the only reward for a mistake, you learn to live with the slow pace.

Ring by ring, clip by clip, I fell into a rhythm and my pace increased. This is where EVA work get really dangerous, too. More than one spacer has gotten a little too comfortable with the process and unclipped his first safety line before clipping his second. In normal space, they end up red-faced with embarrassment as a senior officer chews them out for making the ship waste fuel retrieving them. Inside a wormhole, the spacer quickly drifts into the mist and is never seen again.

Every meter of the way down the hull, I fought the urge to take chances so I could move faster. Every meter of the way down the hull, I concentrated on a simple mantra. Clip the new line. Unclip the old line. Move to the next ring. Clip the new line. Unclip the old line.

It sounds simple, but I was sweating freely by the time I completed the eighty-meter trip down to the cargo hold's emergency airlock. I pulled myself into the airlock and gasped with relief as the horrible voices ceased whispering through my comm. I almost cried with joy as I heard Erica's voice replace them.

"...there, Nancy? Check in as soon as you hear this."

"I'm here, Erica. What's up?"

"I've had the *Darkheart* going through the little maneuvers you programmed into the system, but it hasn't stopped Sam from calling over the comm with questions for you."

I'd forgotten all about the twisting and spinning of the ship during my trek down the hull. I must have concentrated too closely on the clips and rings to notice them. "What did you tell him to put him off?"

"That you were concentrating on the behavior of the inertial dampeners and couldn't be disturbed. He didn't like the answer, but I told him we'd just have to start over again if I interrupted you."

"Good work, Erica. How long did you tell him I'd be busy?"

"Ten minutes, though he's called back every three minutes just to check."

"Hold him off for the full ten minutes and then add an extra half minute as if I was absorbing the test results. Mentioning results, can you cobble together something that looks good and send it to my pad? I'll need something to read off to the asshole if he asks."

"I'm way ahead of you, Nancy. There's an actual dampener system report on your pad now."

The airlock finished cycling and I entered the cargo hold. My headlamp illuminated the closest three crates from among the twenty-six stored in the hold. "Erica, have you got the cargo weights handy? Those ranged all over the place. I thought I'd check the heaviest and then check the lightest if I can get to both of them."

"Hang on, I'll call that up." I heard a buzzing sound through the comm, prompting Erica to mutter, "Screw you, Sam. It hasn't been ten minutes yet."

"That's the intercom?" I asked.

"Yes." The intercom buzzed again. Erica raised her voice, "And the asshole on the other end can wait until I'm good and damned ready to talk to him."

"Tell you what, patch me into the intercom after you find the info on the crates. I'll take the man down a peg or two."

"*I'm* the one stuck up here with the annoying sounds but *you* get to cuss him out? That's not fair, Nancy!"

"Rank hath its privileges," I said.

"Yeah, yeah. I've got your weights. Crates eight, nine, ten, and eleven are the heaviest and crate twenty-six is the lightest."

I checked my packing diagram. "I can get to nine and twenty-six without moving anything. I guess you can go ahead and patch me into the intercom now. I'll talk to Sam while I check out the crates."

Erica was silent for a few seconds. "Okay, you're patched in. Answer any time you want."

As the system buzzed yet again, I keyed open the connection and snapped, "Stop pushing the goddamned button!"

"You weren't answering," Sam replied, his voice tight.

"Because. I. Was. Busy. Like. Erica. Said." I paused just long enough for Sam to draw in breath for his reply and then added, "Do I need to speak more slowly or did the message get through to you?"

"No, I got it. Do I need to remind you who's in charge here?" Polite, hat-in-hand Sam was gone. I'd assumed that man was an act—it looked like I was right. His grammar was better, all of a sudden, too. That was a bit of a surprise.

"I am in charge. My ship. My command. My rules."

"That was before you started going on with these tests and forcing us to strap ourselves into our seats."

I found crate number nine and carefully examined it for an opening mechanism. "Gee, I'm sorry, Sam. If I'd known you wanted to risk the lives of your crew and yourself, I'd have happily skipped the tests. After you signed the cleanup waiver, of course. You can't expect Erica and me to eat the cost of cleaning your molecules off of our bulkheads if the aft inertial dampers fail."

"What I *want* is to come up there and observe this testing you're doing," Sam said.

"No."

"Why not?"

I found a simple locking mechanism. It was coded, of course, but I had a handy FBI decoder device Erica had in her tool box. I put the device against the lock and flicked it on. Lights flashed and characters spun in the display. It all looked very impressive and high tech. I just hoped it worked.

"The really simple reason is there's not enough room up here for an observer while we're doing this. We need to move quickly from reading to reading to ensure everything is working. That means we don't have time to tell some out-of-his-depth freight ape to get out of the way."

"Maybe I know more than you think I do," Sam responded.

"Fine. Tell me what those readings I showed you earlier mean—in detail and using the correct terms—and I'll open the hatch right up."

While Sam sputtered and tried to find something to say in response, the decoder device flashed once and a random series of characters filled the little screen. I pulled it off and carefully entered the code. Putting one hand over the mic for the comm, I pressed enter. With a soft whoosh, the side slid open.

Pulling my hand from the mic, I said, "I don't hear any brilliant explanations, Sam."

"Why don't you explain the readings, then?" Sam shot back.

Within the container was a smaller one, but I immediately recognized the smaller container. What I couldn't figure out was why Miss Perkins and Sam were going to all this trouble to hide portable surgical suites. All Federation navy ships carry a few of these for use during battles or civilian rescue operations. They're expensive, but hardly restricted exports. In fact, the Federation regularly gives these away to new colonies and ones facing medical emergencies.

Backing away from the container, I covered the mic again and closed the container. Puzzled and filled with unexpected trepidation, I headed for container twenty-six.

Sam's voice brought my drifting thoughts back to the here and now. "I said, why don't—"

"I heard you, Sam, but I was busy studying the latest readings—which you interrupted."

"Yeah? Why don't you read that report to me, *Captain*?"

Pulling out my pad, I called up the report. "Fine."

I put as much bored monotone into the reading as possible, speaking loudly enough to cover any minor noises on my end. I was still reading, talking over Sam's attempts to interrupt and shut me up, as the FBI decoder did its work on container twenty-six. Only after I punched in the code and hit enter, did I finally allow Sam to get a word in.

"Okay, stop already!"

"Just doing what you asked, Sam."

"Fine. Whatever. I'm satisfied. How much longer before you're done?"

I shined my headlamp into the container. It revealed a dozen smaller containers stacked in three rows of four. They looked all the world like stasis chambers but were far too small to hold a person. I carefully pulled one out and shined the light through a little window on top of the unit.

"I said, how much longer?" Sam snarled.

I swallowed the bile that crawled up my throat at the sight before me. "Uh, not long. Fifteen minutes, maybe."

"Good. Come get me when you're done."

"Right. I will."

I heard a click and then Erica said, "Okay, Nancy, it's just you and me again." When I didn't respond, she added, "Are you okay? What did you find?"

"Crate twenty-six is filled with small stasis chambers."

"Is it the kids from the school?" Erica asked.

"God, I hope not."

"You're not making any sense, Nancy."

"It's a heart, Erica. The stasis chamber has a human heart in it."

"Damn," Erica muttered, "I hate it when I'm right."

I couldn't keep the incredulity—or the betrayal—out of my voice. "You *expected* this and you didn't even warn me?"

"My superiors disagreed with my analysis and gave me strict orders to keep my theories to myself." I heard the disgust in Erica's voice and could imagine how that conversation went. "Those orders included you, Nancy."

"Okay, we can argue whether you should have obeyed those orders later." I was already repacking the storage crate as I talked. "What I don't understand is why anyone would do this in the first place? Medical nanites can repair almost everything and what they can't repair can be replaced with cloned organs. Why would anyone bother harvesting organs from healthy people? It just doesn't make any sense."

"It makes no sense on Federation worlds—especially the richest and most established ones—but it makes plenty of sense out here on the frontier," Erica said. "But now isn't the time to discuss medical economics. You need to get up here before we run out of wormhole and return to normal space."

"You're right. I'll get started now."

"You've packed everything back the way it was?" Erica asked.

"Of course."

"What about my little decoder unit? You're not leaving that laying around where one of Sam's crew can find it?"

I turned back to crate twenty-six and grabbed the decoder. Zipping it into a pocket, I said, "I'm not stupid, Erica."

"I never thought you were, Nancy, but you've just had a big shock."

"I'm entering the airlock now. And you don't need to worry about me."

"I always worry about the people I work with. I'm just like you in that respect."

I smiled in spite of myself. "Gotcha. See you in ten, Erica."

Then the airlock cycled and I was back in the hell of the wormhole. The mist seemed thicker this time as if it hid giant monsters who waited for just the right moment to pounce. Within seconds, the voices returned, wailing insidiously. Worse, after no more than a minute, the voices began making sense. I'm almost positive my imagination gave them their words, but they gnawed at my gut.

*"Don't leave me in this box!"*

*"I'm all alone!"*

*"What's happening to me?"*

*"It's so dark and so cold!"*

*"I'm scared!"*

*"Why won't you help me?"*

Over and over, the voices cried out to me. Over and over, the voices begged me to stay. Over and over, the voices pleaded for me to help. Over and over, the voices plucked at my conscience. Over and over, the voices tugged at my sanity.

"I'm sorry!" I screamed. "I can't help you!"

"Please, leave me alone!" I cried. "Just leave me alone!"

By the time I pulled myself into the airlock for the pilot's cabin, my breath was coming in gasps. Sweat soaked my clothes. Tears streamed down my face. I was still talking to the voices when the airlock cycled and I fell into the pilot's cabin.

Erica caught me, concern etched on her face. "My God, Nancy, what happened?"

I caught Erica's head between my hands and pulled her face close to mine. My voice nothing but a harsh whisper, I said, "Tell me we're going to stop these bastards. Tell me we're going to get vengeance for everyone they've...they've..."

Erica pulled me into a tight hug. "Yes, Nancy. We're going to make the bastards pay. We're going to make every last one of them pay and pay and pay."

# CHAPTER THREE

As much as Erica and I wanted to spend the next who-knows-how-long coming to grips with the horror I found in the hold, we couldn't afford that luxury. After one more quick squeeze, my partner began unfastening the EVA harness while I wiped my eyes and made myself as presentable as possible.

We weren't a minute too soon, as the intercom buzzed seconds after we finished. I ignored it and stepped to the hatch. Mid-buzz, I toggled the hatch and it slid into the bulkhead with a soft hiss. A surprised Sam looked up from the call button.

I thrust my face a couple of centimeters from his and barked, "What?"

The guy must have never gone through boot camp because he recoiled and fell back a couple of steps. Those steps carried Sam onto Lloyd's toes, who yelped and shoved Sam forward again. At the same time, I took another step toward Sam, trapping the crew boss between me and his crew member.

"I asked you a question, Sam." I kept my tone sharp and annoyed. "What is so damned important it couldn't wait until we finished our tests? What do you have to ask me that is more important than your lives?"

Finding himself on the defensive, Sam stuttered, "Well, I... Uh, that is...Um."

"Is this your idea of a joke? Bug us and bug us and bug us and, when I finally have time to respond to you, you've got nothing?" I shook my head in disgust and turned back toward the pilot's compartment. "If you were in the navy, I'd flay you alive for this."

The man finally found his tongue. "Well, I'm not in your damned navy and neither are you anymore. This isn't a navy ship. You work for Miss Perkins and, on this trip, that means you answer to me."

I spun around to face Sam again. "Oh really? Fine, let's pretend what you said is the way of the world. What is it you want, O mighty leader? Why have you been buzzing the intercom incessantly for twenty minutes or more?"

"I want to examine the ship's logs, including the automated systems logs."

I hesitated, unsure if Erica had scrubbed the system logs of all evidence of my trip down the outside of the ship. Fortunately, she called out, "Send him in, Nancy. I'll keep an eye on him so you can take a break."

We exited the wormhole while Sam was studying the logs. Erica handled the piloting since I was in my cabin. As expected, she didn't have much to do except punch in the course for the next wormhole. Faced with a twenty-hour transit before our next jump, Sam's crew quickly grew bored and returned to the vid player. Sam spent a few hours watching us like a hawk before getting bored himself. By the midway point in our trip across the system, everyone was leaving Erica and me alone. We still waited until our ten passengers were sleeping before discussing our grisly cargo.

Erica and I made small talk while my partner scanned the pilot's compartment for any recently-planted listening devices. We'd left the compartment open since exiting the wormhole, so Sam or one of his crew could have easily left a surprise for us. Neither of us thought it was likely, though, and we were right.

Confident we could talk openly, I positioned myself so I could see down the corridor leading to our hatch. Cradling a blaster set to stun, I said, "You promised to tell me why organ harvesting makes sense for frontier colonies."

Erica nodded, "When I first thought of that as a possibility, I performed an economic analysis to make sure it was feasible before presenting my theory to the agent in charge of the investigation."

"Did they disagree with your assessment?"

"No, they commended me for being thorough but thought the slavery angle was more economically lucrative." Erica paused, marshaling her thoughts. "How much do you know about medical nanites and medical cloning?"

I shrugged. "About what anyone knows. Nanites can repair all sorts of damage, ranging from removing diseased cells to rebuilding organs and tissue. Sometimes, the damage is too extensive. That's where cloning comes in. I never gave it much thought."

"You're not alone in that, Nancy. Hell, I was no different until this case came along." Erica sighed and leaned forward. "Are you aware that all nanites have their own special programming? Trauma nanites swarm to the source of the greatest damage and perform a stop-gap repair. Essentially, stabilizing the patient for more exacting medical procedures in a hospital. Surgical nanites are all specialized, meaning a nanite programmed to repair a heart is of no use for liver repairs."

"Okay, that makes sense."

"Did you also know that nanites are never reprogrammed?" I shook my head and Erica continued, "It's a safety concern. Can you imagine what could happen if the new code didn't completely replace the old, if some residual heart-repair commands remained in a nanite reprogrammed to work on the lungs? The risks are minuscule, but when you're reprogramming millions of nanites for a single procedure, chances are very good some of the nanites will have problems. But nanites are easy to get, so no one worries about it."

"Which was my point," I said.

"Let me modify that. Nanites are easy to get in the Federation. They require exacting manufacturing processes, an almost-paranoid level of quality control, and they deteriorate rapidly. No one uses nanites that are more than six months old. But on any kind of established world—like all member planets of the Federation—the population is large enough to support the nanite industry and ensure the vast majority of the nanites produced are actually used."

"Why not just put them in stasis until they're needed?" I asked.

"Nanites don't respond well to stasis. They actually degrade faster inside a stasis chamber than they do normally. I don't understand the technical explanation for it, so you'll just have to take my word on this."

"So, frontier worlds don't have the manufacturing capability to produce nanites, much less the population to use the nanites if they did," I said. "And importing nanites is expensive and impractical because too many of them will degrade before they're used."

"Right. Without going into unnecessary details, organ cloning faces many of the same obstacles," Erica replied. "But organ transplants are easy. The required drugs are cheap and easy to produce and you can perform a transplant in something as simple as an emergency surgical suite."

I lowered my head into my hands. "All you need is the organs."

"Exactly."

"Since we've got a hold full of organs, that means the... harvesting...is probably done back on Osnade," I said. "Why don't we turn around and head back there now?"

"I want to at least make the first delivery. While Sam and his crew is busy offloading stuff, I'm going to sneak out and see if I can find some records to help us narrow down our search of Osnade."

"Why? Just bring in a naval task force and bring their sensors to bear on the problem."

Erica gave me an incredulous look. "Are you trying to start a war, Nancy?"

"Oh, crap, I forgot. Osnade isn't a member of the Federation. That's going to make things a lot harder. Do you think we can count on help from the Osnade government?"

"Maybe. But we have to have rock-solid evidence for that. Even with that, the Osnadian government is going to be very upset that the FBI ran an operation so far outside of our jurisdiction."

"Okay, Erica, we'll play this straight until we make the first delivery and can gather some evidence."

Erica and I kept things quiet for the rest of the trip to our first delivery. We didn't mess with any readings or go out of our way to antagonize the freight handlers. Mind you, we didn't give them access to our cabins no matter how much they complained about crowding. You've got to have *some* standards when you own the ship, after all. But we took our turns prepping meals, cleaning up afterward, and handling basic cleaning chores on the ship. If Sam's crew appreciated our efforts, they didn't say anything.

Two days later, we made the final wormhole jump into the Tokra system. That wormhole was the shortest I'd ever traveled through—we were in and out in less than twenty minutes—but it's the distance saved in a wormhole that matters, not how long it takes to traverse it. The Tokra wormhole covered eight light-years in that short time.

Traffic around Tokra was light, with no more than a dozen starships in the system, when we arrived. There were a few hundred local ships—almost certainly unequipped for wormhole transit—moving about on unknown business. Most of them were ore haulers or mining ships, since Tokra has a large asteroid belt filled with valuable mineral deposits.

The actual planet of Tokra wasn't heavily settled. It's a tropical world with what are supposed to be crystal clear oceans and a colorful array of sea life. If the planet was closer to the Federation, it would probably be a prime destination for the extremely wealthy looking for the ultimate get-away. Instead, the planet houses rest and relaxation facilities for the miners and their families, as well as a few dozen mansions belonging to the owners of the mining companies. To my surprise, the owners' estates were down among the R&R locations. I'd have thought the owners would stay as far away from the hoi polloi as possible.

Once we finished getting our bearings in the system, I called Sam to the pilot's compartment. When he arrived, I said, "Time to cough up our landing coordinates, Sam."

"We ain't landing," he said, pulling out his pocket pad. He showed me a set of coordinates. "We dock here."

I brought them up on the system map and was surprised to see we weren't going anywhere near the planet. So much for a lazy night on the tropical planet. I zoomed in on the map and found a mining base built in a played-out asteroid. That was unexpected. I examined the readout for the base.

"Looks like we just dock on the outside of that thing?" When Sam nodded, I continued, "Do you know if they've got artificial gravity inside or does the asteroid spin along its axis? It matters for docking."

"I know why you asked. This ain't my first run, Captain." It suddenly dawned on me that less-than-grammatical-Sam was back. Was this just an act he dropped into, something so ingrained he didn't even notice? I filed that aside as a question for another day as Sam said, "Artificial gravity. Shouldn't be no problem docking since the asteroid won't be spinning."

"Good enough, Sam. You and the crew can relax. I'll have us docked in a couple of hours, give or take a few minutes."

Studying the course to the base, Sam quirked an eyebrow. "That's kinda quick, what with all them other asteroids out there, ain't it?"

I knew I could fly the course in half of that time with the *Darkheart*—a quarter of the time in my old starfighter—and thought my projected course time was terribly slow. Everyone in the galaxy thinks asteroid fields are death traps—top-notch pilots excepted. I blame adventure vids and virt games for that misconception.

I smirked at Sam. "Just don't look out of the windows, grandpa, and you won't feel a thing."

"And the reason you won't feel a thing," Erica said, "is the alignment job we did on the inertial dampeners."

I jerked a thumb at my partner. "What she said."

Sam huffed a nonverbal response and headed aft. Once he was out of sight, I settled into my seat and grinned at Erica.

"You mind if I give them a scary show by swinging close to a few of the smaller asteroids?"

The other woman looked uneasy at the thought. "Uh, you don't have to show off to impress me, Nancy."

That's when I remembered she was a pilot, but not Fed Navy-trained. Hell, she wasn't even Fringer Navy-trained. Her thoughts on asteroid fields probably aligned more with Sam than with me.

I leaned toward her, lowering my voice. "Let me tell you a secret, Erica. This isn't as dangerous as the vids and games make it seem. I could fly through this field in a little over an hour just using the ship's instruments and not even break a sweat. Trust me."

Erica gave an uncertain nod of her head. "Then why all the play-acting with Sam?"

"The number one unwritten rule of piloting is we never, ever, tell non-pilots it's easy. It ruins the 'daring pilot' mystique and usually lowers the pay rate, to boot. Besides, it's always fun to impress the rubes." I glanced over my shoulder, down the corridor toward the ship's common area. "Beyond that, it's a good idea to keep something in reserve when dealing with scum like Sam and his crew."

With Erica's agreement, I plotted a fun little course with three close fly-bys. Those asteroids never intersected our course, but from the sphincter-clenching cries coming from the common area Sam's crew never figured that out. I also docked the *Darkheart* exactly two hours after Sam went aft.

Several members of Sam's crew were still pale from our trip to the base and, to my considerable delight, one of the women was on her way to change clothes. I don't know if she didn't clench her sphincter tightly enough or if her bladder just let go, but I took it as a good omen.

"What do we do now that we're docked, Sam?" I asked.

"I say we never let you pilot this ship again," Wanda spat, glaring at me.

"You're more than welcome to stay here when we leave because nobody except me pilots the *Darkheart*." I met her glare with a tight smile and folded arms.

Wanda waved a hand at Erica. "She piloted when we came out of that first wormhole. Don't see why she can't pilot when we leave here."

"I plugged courses into the autopilot, nothing more," Erica said. "Yeah, I can pilot the ship in an emergency, but this isn't an emergency."

"But—"

"Shaddup, Wanda," Sam growled. He turned to me and answered my initial question. "We head to the cargo hold and get our delivery ready to go. That means *all* of us."

I shook my head. "I want Erica at the controls monitoring our load balance."

"Jesus, woman, we done balanced the damn load!" Sam said, his voice rising an octave.

"Jesus, man, that was on Osnade," I said, raising my voice an octave, too.

"So, what?"

"So, we're going to remove some of that carefully balanced cargo. That's going to put it *out* of balance again."

"You didn't think of that back on Osnade?"

"Yes, Sam, I thought of it on Osnade, but it's impossible to balance a load like this so it's good after each delivery. You want that, you bring me absolutely identical crates next time."

"They *are* the same!"

"But they don't have the same *mass*. Please tell me you understand the difference." I pulled out my pad and accessed the listed weight of each crate, "All you have to do is compare crate eleven, which masses one point one six metric tons at earth-normal gravity, with crate twenty-six, which masses one hundred and thirty-six kilos, to see what I mean."

Sam just folded his arms and glared at me. I don't really think he cared one way or the other about rebalancing the cargo, he was just tired of losing every argument with me. Too bad, because he was about to lose this one, too.

"Fine," I shrugged. "We'll leave everything where it is after unloading and I'll *try* to keep the ship stable when we fly back out of the asteroid field."

Nine voices were raised in protest at that, led by Wanda. The woman changing her pants was so perturbed by the idea she ran back to add her voice while she was still naked from the waist down. It says something about how upset the crew was that none of the men noticed.

"All right!" Sam shouted. "Shaddup, all of ya. We'll rebalance the damn cargo."

I'd just bought Erica a good four or five hours she could use to infiltrate this mining base.

While I oversaw unloading the cargo, Erica tried tying her pocket pad into the load balancer display. Neither of us held much hope for that, since the display was never designed to broadcast. What would be the purpose of that since any crew member could monitor it directly? Of course, we wanted Erica both free to leave the ship *and* able to give me periodic load balance reports. In the end, she simply pointed one of the many ship's surveillance cams at the display and linked her pocket pad display to the cam.

The set-up wasn't perfect, but it only had to fool Sam and his collection of mental midgets for a few hours. Besides, they were going to be too busy shifting cargo around on the whim of their crazy captain to worry about Erica.

By the time we—and by we, I mean Sam and his crew supervised by me—finished shifting the cargo onto the dock, representatives from the client arrived. Perfunctory introductions were given and, with one exception, promptly forgotten by all. The one exception was Dr. Spinnock, who I assume was on hand to examine the merchandise.

That assumption proved correct when the foreman of the local crew said, "Okay, open 'em up so the doc can check out the cargo."

Sam looked at me and said, "Go to the pilot's compartment, Captain. I'll send someone for you when we're ready to rebalance the cargo."

Noting the return of grammatical Sam, I shoved off of the bulkhead I'd been leaning against and sauntered into the ship.

I didn't want Sam or any of his crew coming all the way to the pilot's compartment and discovering Erica wasn't there, so said over my shoulder, "My cabin is more comfortable. Look for me there."

I watched the gears in Sam's head spin as he worked out that my cabin was on the other side of the ship from the cargo hatch. Since he just wanted me somewhere I couldn't spy on the inspection, my cabin should be fine. I half expected Sam to insist on getting his way, but I guess he wanted to look somewhat professional to the customers.

"That's fine, Captain," he said, already turning away from me.

For the next hour, I kept up with Erica's progress inside the mining base. After slipping through the same airlock I used for my harrowing wormhole EVA, she had little trouble finding an unused docking bay and slipping inside the base. From there, things got more difficult for her. We didn't have access to any interior designs and were simply hoping Erica could figure out where to go from signs or consoles or whatever they used in mining bases.

The base used your basic colored lines and actually painted them on the walls. Most Federation facilities use lighted strips, but we were well outside of the Federation. I assume it's a safety thing, so people can find their way even in a power blackout. The difficulty wasn't following the lines, it was figuring out what each color represented.

Erica's sigh of frustration was clear even over our low-gain connection. "I'm going to follow the red line and hope red is for medical."

She followed various red lines for much longer than either of us thought reasonable. Finally, she spied a major corridor down a side tunnel and headed for it. That's when Nate popped his head into my cabin.

"Sam says you can come back now."

Swinging my legs off my bunk, I said, "Be still, my racing heart."

"Huh?"

"My excitement knows no bounds," I replied. "I am all aflutter with excitement."

"Whatever," Nate muttered, heading back to the cargo hold.

Dr. Spinnock, the freight crew, and the freight were all gone when we got to the hold. I took a few minutes examining the load distribution, making mental notes where I actually wanted everything to end up. I'd already worked this out in advance, something that never occurred to Sam and company.

"Okay, Erica, give me the load balance readings as they stand now."

There was a longer than anticipated pause before Erica gave me the readings. She followed that by saying, "Sorry, Captain, I was in the head. It won't happen again."

"See that it doesn't, Erica." Turning to Sam, I said, "Okay, let's start over here with crates nine and ten."

For the next several hours, I ran the crew ragged. They moved every single one of the remaining twenty-two crates at least twice, most of them four or five times. Much as I wanted updates on Erica's progress, I couldn't ask for them with everyone crowded around me. With the crew dripping sweat and saving their breath for panting, I knew I'd pushed them as far as I could. Hoping my partner had found what we wanted, I gave her the code phrase to get back to the ship.

"Okay, folks, we're getting very close. I think this next shift will get it."

Erica gave her acknowledging phrase right on queue. "Thank God, Captain. It's exhausting sitting up here watching that display."

As expected, Sam's crew voiced some less than sympathetic opinions of Erica and her exhaustion. I got them right to work, giving them no chance to build up any real animosity for Erica. The last thing I needed was one of these idiots deciding to beat some sense—or the crew's idea of sense—into her.

Fifteen minutes later, Sam's comm buzzed. Looking surprised, he moved out of his crew's way and answered the comm. I'm sure I was at least as curious as Sam was about the call. Had the customers found some defective...'parts' doesn't seem like the right word when you're talking about human organs, but what else was there? I squelched my questions and concentrated on directing the crew. I didn't hear the man close the call.

"Please be so kind, Captain Martin," said grammatical Sam, "to turn around very slowly."

I did as instructed and found Sam's blaster pointed at my chest.

It's never fun staring down the business end of a blaster, but this wasn't the first time for me. People like Sam are the same all over—they're looking for fear. They get off on it. They feed on it. They get bolder. And, too often, they end up doing something really stupid, such as shooting the person staring down the business end of the blaster.

I was all for Sam doing something stupid, just not if that something ended up with me dead. So I kept my face impassive, folded my arms, canted my hips, and raised one eyebrow.

"I thought you were in a hurry, Sam."

I was rewarded with a look of confusion that flitted across Sam's face. He got control of himself pretty quickly, but it was obvious the confrontation wasn't going the way he expected.

"Call your partner and tell her to come back here."

Crap. Someone on the base must have caught Erica. None of the crew from the base saw her during the unloading, so if a resident spotted her heading back here they wouldn't automatically know she was a stranger. But if they caught her and couldn't identify her, that would point right at the only ship currently docked at the base—the *Darkheart*.

Erica and I had a plan for this, but it was tenuous at best. Part one of the plan was for me to play dumb.

Shrugging as if Sam's request wasn't a big deal, I tapped my comm. "Erica, can you come back to the cargo hold for a minute?"

I waited a few seconds and then tried again. "Erica? This is extremely unfunny—like blaster-pointed-at-my-chest levels of unfunny."

After a few more seconds, I rolled my eyes and then met Sam's gaze. "You want me to go up front and look for her or do you want to send one of your crew?"

"There's no need for anyone to look for her," Sam said. "Someone else is already bringing her back to the ship."

"What do you mean, *back* to the ship? She's probably just in the head."

Sam shook his head. "Your partner left the ship hours ago."

"She was caught inside the base?" At Sam's nod, I did my best to look furious. "Son. Of. A. Bitch! I can't believe she's doing this crap again."

"What crap?" Sam looked truly puzzled as the scene followed a different script than the one he expected.

"I took Erica on as a favor to a friend. Call her a reclamation project. She was a thief growing up, straightened out for a while in the Fringer Navy, but fell back to thievery after her husband died." I shook my head sadly. "A friend thought she'd respond well if she was working with another war vet who lost someone near and dear."

"And that's supposed to be you?"

This is the point where most people nod in understanding, so I didn't have to fake my expression of astonishment. "Yes, me. Captain Nancy Martin of the Terran Federation Navy. Assigned to the *TFS Phoenix*. Fighter Squadron three oh eight."

"I've never heard of you."

"What about the *Ark 2*. Does that ring any bells?"

"Nope." Sam looked at his crew, "Does that mean anything to any of you?"

Heads shook 'no' all around me. I'd been searching for someplace where every other person didn't ask me about the battle with the insane AI Arktu or offered sympathy for the loss of Sko. Apparently, I just didn't go out far enough until this trip.

"Whatever. The point is, I've kept Erica on a tight leash so she can't wander off and get into trouble. That's why I had her in the pilot's compartment giving me cargo balance readings." I screwed my face up in puzzlement. "And she was doing that, too. How the hell did she manage that *and* slip off the ship?"

Watching me, Sam lowered his blaster. He didn't holster it, but at least he wouldn't blow a hole between my breasts if his finger twitched unexpectedly. At the same time, a couple of men from the mining station dragged Erica into the docking bay. Dr. Spinnock trailed along behind them.

My partner lifted her head, an undoubtedly real expression of remorse on her face. "I'm sorry, Nancy, I—"

Sam stepped over and slapped Erica hard. "Silence! I'll tell you when you can speak."

Dr. Spinnock frowned at the scene but didn't comment on it. "We caught her slipping out of the medical records room. I can't imagine what she was doing in there since we don't keep anything of value among the records."

Sam grabbed Erica by the hair and jerked her head up to face him. "Explain yourself."

"I...I got lost. I was looking for shops so I could lift a little something. A souvenir, you know?" Erica tried to shrug, not an easy thing to do with a man holding each of her arms and Sam pulling on her hair. "When I found the records room, I thought maybe I could find some receiving records and maybe get the door number for a storeroom."

Sam motioned for a couple of his crew to take Erica from the men holding her. "Put her in her cabin. I'll take care of her once I finish here."

"Don't be too harsh on the woman," Dr. Spinnock said. "She did no real damage. In fact, she was remarkably neat, leaving the records exactly as she found them."

"She did considerable damage to our reputation," Sam growled.

"No, Sam," I said, "she damaged *my* reputation. Members of my crew are my responsibility." I turned to the doctor. "Thank you for returning her to us. May I repay you for your time and effort?"

Dr. Spinnock waved off my offer, "There's no need, Captain Martin. It gave our security team a much-needed real-life test."

"That's very kind of you, sir," I said, extending my hand.

The man took my hand, eying me curiously. "That young woman called you Nancy. You aren't *the* Captain Nancy Martin of *Ark 2* fame, are you?"

I ducked my head, embarrassed despite myself. "That was a lifetime ago, Dr. Spinnock. These days I'm just plain old Captain Martin."

"I think I understand, Captain—at least as well as anyone who wasn't there *can* understand." The man added his second hand to our clasp and flashed a brief smile. "Let me just say, I thank the Creator there are people like you in this universe."

With that, the doctor and his two companions turned and left.

"What was that all about?" Wanda asked no one in particular.

"It don't matter," ungrammatical Sam spat. "We done wasted enough time on this crap. Get yer asses onboard."

I ignored Sam, watching the doctor's retreating back until he entered a tunnel and was lost from sight. What could cause a man like that to do business with someone like Miss Perkins? I simply couldn't reconcile the man's words, his caring tone of voice, and the look in his eyes with people who would kidnap young people just to harvest their organs.

"Hey, Captain Hero," Sam called from inside the ship, "get a move on. We got a schedule to keep."

Suddenly, I wanted nothing more than to have a very long talk with Dr. Spinnock. As I followed Sam into the ship, I began concocting a plan that might let me do just that. It was a desperate plan, but it couldn't be any worse than going to war against an insane AI and his robot army. Could it?

Deep in thought, I closed the cargo hatch and entered the ship proper. And there was Sam, pointing his blaster at me again.

I heaved a dramatic sigh and said, "This is getting old, Sam."

"You better get used to it, Captain, 'cause you gonna see it a lot."

"Why?"

"Why you think? Yeah, you and yer partner got an explanation fer her slippin' out of the ship, but just cause the doc out there bought it don't mean I did."

This version of ungrammatical Sam was even less grammatical than any of the previous versions. It was getting too confusing to keep up with it anymore.

"Why do you do that, Sam?"

"Do what?"

"Speak perfectly intelligible, grammatically correct gal base when you're talking to customers and then fall into some level of gutter grammar when they're gone? I mean, you're not even consistently ungrammatical. It makes you look stupid." I considered that for a moment, then added, "Well, *more* stupid."

"We're not talking about my speech patterns, okay? We're talking about your partner leaving the ship under mysterious circumstances and just how much you know about it."

I smiled and nodded. "That's much better, Sam. Maybe you should just stick to speaking properly. At least you can maintain some consistency that way."

Sam's face turned red. "Shut up and hand me your blaster."

Deciding I'd pushed the man as far as was safe right now, I carefully unbuckled my gun belt and passed it to him. "You do realize you still need me to pilot the ship?"

"Yeah, but you don't need your partner to help. She said as much earlier."

"No, she said she could pilot in emergencies, not that I don't need her help. Who do you think handles the navigation?"

"But you can do the navigation if you have to, right?"

"Yes, Sam, but it will take longer and throw off your precious delivery schedule."

"Maybe, but I think I'll be able to trust you better if you know pretty Erica's life is forfeit if you don't follow my orders exactly."

"Life is forfeit? That's a fancy turn of phrase, Sam. Come on, admit it, you've never been a street thug, have you? Hell, I bet you've even got a college degree."

"Look, Captain, do you understand the situation? Your partner is going to be tied down to her bed so she can't get into any trouble. If you don't follow orders, I'll let the men in the crew...play...with Erica. Things will only get worse from there. Do. You. Understand?"

Damn, I was right earlier. I pushed Sam just a bit too far with the grammar jibes. "Yes, Sam, I understand perfectly. I follow your instructions to the letter or Erica suffers."

"Good. Now let's get up to the pilot's compartment and find out how she kept up with the load balance readings when she wasn't even in the ship."

Of course, Erica's set up was obvious once Sam spent a couple of minutes examining the compartment. He grabbed Erica's pad just to be sure, which gave me a chance to see her. She was very efficiently tied spread-eagled on the bed.

"You okay, kid?" I asked while Sam pawed through her pockets.

"Yeah. I'm just sorry I got you in trouble."

"Don't sweat it. We'll get this all worked out in the end. Everything will be fine."

Sam came up with the pad and smirked at me as he pushed me out of the cabin. "You could be right, Captain. I will say Miss Perkins will be much more understanding of the situation if the rest of our deliveries go off without a hitch."

"I figured that one out all by myself, Sam."

"Good. Then it's time we were leaving this base."

Sam followed me all the way to the pilot's compartment and settled comfortably into Erica's seat. He kept his blaster handy in his lap.

"It wouldn't be a very good idea to shoot me, Sam. Who would you get to fly the ship if I was dead?"

"It's set to stun, Captain, but I'm also certain we could find a replacement pilot here. They've got hundreds of ships flying around the system, after all."

"Maybe, but in-system ships aren't the same as starships nor do you pilot them the same way."

"Yeah, whatever, but I really think Erica is the only insurance I need against your good behavior."

"*I* haven't misbehaved at all, Sam, so I don't see what you're worried about."

"You haven't, but you're the one who wanted your partner in the pilot's compartment instead of helping us with the cargo. For all I know, the two of you are in this together and searching medical records is your way of trying to find out about the cargo you're transporting."

That was disturbingly close to the truth. But it also gave me an idea.

"You might be right about Erica. This is her first cargo run and Miss Perkins' tight-lipped never-you-mind attitude probably piqued her curiosity. From there, it's easy for her imagination to turn it into something fascinating and valuable." Absently, I buckled myself into my seat while catching Sam's gaze with my own. "If you really want to keep the cargo secret, make up a list of boring-but-useful stuff. Wave that around, drop the top-secret routine, and chances are no one on a ship's crew will give the cargo a second thought."

"I'll remember to tell Miss Perkins that when we get back," Sam said as he buckled into his seat's harness. "It's a good suggestion."

"Just remember to tell her who suggested it and how well I behaved." I brought the engines online and got departure clearance from the mining base. Toggling the ship's intercom, I said, "We're ready for departure."

"Let's keep it nice and easy leaving, okay?" Sam said. "None of that crap you pulled coming in."

"Roger that, Sam." I used the intercom again to announce, "Your boss ordered me to take it easy on the way out. You can all relax your sphincters."

A mixture of laughter and insults drifted up the corridor and through the open hatch. Sam added a chuckle as I nosed the *Darkheart* away from the mining station and took a wide, gentle turn back toward the edge of the asteroid field and the course toward the wormhole. For the next several hours, I flew nice and easy, never once coming close to any of the asteroids.

I keyed the intercom again as we exited the field. "We're clear of the asteroids, everyone."

A couple of Sam's people raised brief cheers. Sam unbuckled his harness, stood up, and stretched. As he arched his back and neck, his eyes were briefly looking straight up. Without hesitation, I turned off every inertial dampener on the ship and shoved the throttle wide open.

# CHAPTER FOUR

With a startled squawk, Sam slammed back into the co-pilot's seat. Arched back as he was before I hit the throttle, the top of his head hit the seat's headrest and snapped down as his neck and body folded into the chair.

"What the hell?" Sam said. Then something snapped with an audible crack. "Aaaahhh!"

From down the corridor, I heard lots of thumps and shouts as the rest of Sam's crew tumbled around in the living area. Next to me, Sam fumbled with his blaster, trying to bring it up to aim at me.

With a savage grin at the man, I reversed thrust. That is not something any sane pilot does with a civilian engine running at maximum thrust. It's a great way to break all sorts of expensive parts, void warranties, and otherwise destroy your engine. Military engines, on the other hand, are designed for this sort of thing. It's written right into the specs because combat maneuvers often require several wild changes in thrust every minute. There are reasons military engines cost about a hundred times more than the equivalent civilian engines and this level of mechanical tolerance is the single biggest one.

With the inertial dampeners still offline, the effects of reversing thrust were spectacular. While I felt my safety harness press deeply into my body, Sam flew forward and smashed face first into the co-pilot's control panel. Blood splashed from what was certainly a broken nose. He probably had a few broken teeth, too. I heard crashing, cursing, and a couple of agonized screams from the rest of the freight crew.

I pulled the thrust to neutral and all of the pressure vanished. My right hand snaked out and grabbed the blaster away from a badly-dazed Sam. Then I pushed the man out of the co-pilot's seat.

"That's reserved for my friend, asshole!"

Sam landed on the deck, right in front of the corridor to the rest of the ship. Once again, I shoved the throttle wide open. As the ship's acceleration pressed me deeply into my seat, I heard Sam give an inarticulate cry as he slid through the hatch and bounced down the corridor to join his crew.

When I heard the freight crew boss stop moving, I cut thrust entirely. Then, with what I imagine was a gleam of anticipation in my eyes, I hit my harness quick-release and turned off the artificial gravity. Making sure the blaster was set to stun, I shoved off down the corridor.

I used every handhold and protrusion to pull myself along as fast as possible. Just before the end of the corridor, I reversed my position, rebounded off the wall with both feet and sailed into the living area.

It was a mess. The furniture was still in place, but only because it was permanently fastened to the deck. Vid boxes, cups, plates, entertainment pads, and the ten-person freight crew were thrown all around the room. They looked like my niece's toys after she threw a particularly nasty tantrum.

Several of the crew lay unmoving while the rest groaned and tried to get their bearings. Every single one of them looked like they were in considerable pain. Never let it be said that Nancy Martin isn't merciful. As I glided over them, I took careful aim and stunned each of them with a shot from the blaster. It was quite therapeutic—for me.

"Um, is that you, Nancy?" Erica called from her cabin.

I reversed direction against a wall and flew majestically into my partner's room. "Who else would it be, kid?"

"You do realize I'm a year older than you?" Erica asked.

I began untying my partner. "You do realize there's more to being the 'kid' than age?"

"I do now, O Wise One." Erica rubbed her wrists for a few seconds before sitting up and helping me free her feet. "Last I saw, Sam had you covered with a blaster. Can I assume all that jerking back and forth was you turning the tables on him?"

"Yep. The silly man thought a handgun gave him the edge over a pilot armed with an entire spaceship."

When we drifted out into the living area, Erica gave a low whistle at the sight. "Remind me to never get on your bad side. So, what's the plan now?"

"We need to secure Sam and his crew. After that, I want to have a long talk with Dr. Spinnock from the mining base."

"Then what? Our original idea of infiltrating ourselves into the organization is pretty thoroughly shot."

"Yeah, but I never liked that plan. Gaining trust and infiltrating criminal organizations takes time—and that's time those school kids don't have." I shrugged. "I guess we're just going to have to make it up as we go."

Erica grinned at me. "In that case, I can't think of anyone else I'd rather have as my partner."

I grinned back. "Same here, kid."


A little less than an hour later, I turned the artificial gravity on again and placed a call to the mining base. It took a few minutes, but eventually Dr. Spinnock's face appeared on the comm screen.

"Hello again, Captain Martin. I thought you'd be in the wormhole by now."

"Dr. Spinnock, I have some questions for you and then some news you absolutely must hear." The doctor inclined his head in acknowledgment, so I asked, "What is the source of the body parts you took delivery of today?"

The doctor's genial expression vanished. "I was told others would try to interrupt and intercept these deliveries. I never thought it would be someone like *you*, Captain Martin. I am sorely disappointed."

As answers go, that was both illuminating and confusing. "My interest has nothing to do with intercepting deliveries, sir, though I do admit it has everything to do with interrupting them."

"Do you have any idea just how dangerous mining is, Captain?" Anger formed in the doctor's eyes. "Even the simplest of injuries can result in lost limbs or irreparably damaged organs. Unlike the worlds of the Federation, we cannot maintain cloning or medical nanite facilities. We depend on the generosity of grief-stricken families all across the galaxy, people who allow the harvesting of limbs and organs from recently deceased loved ones. People who put their concern for others above their concern for keeping their deceased loved ones—"

"Stop it, doctor." I scrubbed a hand over my face. "Just... stop it."

"I will *not* stop, Captain Martin! These donations—"

"The limbs and organs are *not* donations!" I'd meant to work up to this slowly, but the doctor's words and tone made me act impulsively. "No one offered those parts out of concern for you. Dammit, no one *offered* those parts at all! You've been dealing with criminals who kidnap healthy, happy young people, cut them up for parts, and sell the parts to naive idiots like you!"

I pulled out my pad and called up the photo of the kids who disappeared on their school trip. I held it up so it would display on the doctor's comm screen. "My partner and I are trying to find the people behind this before those bastards butcher every last one of these kids."

The blood drained from the doctor's face and his mouth opened and closed several times before he found his voice. "Merciful God in Heaven...I...I didn't know."

I lowered my voice and put all of the sympathy I currently felt for the man into my voice. "I know you didn't, Dr. Spinnock. That's why we're asking for your help. You're the only person we know who has dealt with them."

"I'll do everything I can, of course, but I'm not the one who negotiated for the dona—." The man caught himself halfway through the word and buried his face in his hands. "What have we done?"

"You couldn't know, Dr. Spinnock," I said. "But if you didn't do the negotiations, who did?"

"The owner of our mining company. He lives on Tokra. Let me contact him and arrange a meeting."


Forty minutes later, armed with landing coordinates for the company owner's estate, I set course for the tropical planet of Tokra.

Two high-end flitters were waiting for us when we landed at the spaceport on Tokra. A chauffeur stood outside the first car. Four well-armed guards stood outside the second.

Eying the guards, Erica said under her breath, "Is our host so unpopular that even his guests need an armed escort?"

As one of the guards strode briskly toward us, I said, "I guess we're about to find out."

The man stopped in front of us and extended a hand. "I'm Captain Rollins of the Tokra Security Force."

I took his hand and gave it a perfunctory pump. "Captain Nancy Martin, here, and this is my partner, Erica Hampton."

"It's an honor to meet you, ma'am," Rollins said to me. He took Erica's hand for a quick shake and gave her an acknowledging nod. "Ma'am."

"Are we in any danger, Captain Rollins?" my partner asked. "You've brought an awful lot of firepower just to escort us to your boss's estate."

"We work for the planetary government, Miss Hampton, not Titan Mining. Nor are we here to escort you to your meeting with Mr. Malla." The captain gestured to the *Darkheart,* "Mr. Malla contacted us after speaking with one of his doctors. He told us you have some criminals onboard. We're here to transport them to a secure holding facility, if you don't mind."

Erica and I had already decided one of us would stay with the prisoners to act as guard, but this offer put a different spin on things. Since Erica is the one trained in criminal matters, I motioned for her to field the Captain's request.

"Do your laws allow you to hold them without filing charges?" she asked.

"No, but I understand they are part of an illegal organ trafficking operation. We can hold them for a very long time on those charges alone." Captain Rollins hesitated for a few seconds, then said, "May I request your official involvement in this affair? It's for our records and will be kept on a need-to-know basis."

"I am Special Agent Erica Hampton of the Federation Bureau of Investigation. I recruited Captain Martin to assist in an undercover operation to find the source of these organs and, we desperately hope, save as many of the young people taken by these bastards as possible."

"Thank you, Special Agent Hampton. I'll forgo jurisdictional reminders and instead wish you the best of luck taking down those bastards." He motioned to the ship, "With your permission, we'll take those criminals off your hands. Rest assured, you can have them back anytime you want them."

At Erica's nod, Captain Rollins and his three-man team boarded the *Darkheart*.

"That went surprisingly well," Erica said as we walked to the other car. "I don't usually get that level of cooperation from local law enforcement when I'm working in the Federation. I expected outright hostility this far outside of my jurisdiction."

"Surely all lawmen will put aside such minor concerns when a few hundred kids' lives are on the line," I said.

"You'd think." Erica didn't elaborate on that.

We reached the waiting flitter and slid into the back seat. The chauffeur immediately took to the air, noting local points of interest during our fifteen-minute flight.

He landed on the grounds of a vast estate. Colorful gardens brightened a wide, green lawn. Fifty meters away from our landing spot, at least a hundred teenagers milled around a huge swimming pool. Some swam, some played games in the pool, some danced to music from a live band, and some just chatted up members of the opposite sex. A few adults stood on the fringe of the party, several of them manning grills. The smell of cooking meat wafted our way, reminding me that I'd eaten nothing but ship's rations for the last week.

"Let me guess," I said, "it's Mr. Malla's daughter's birthday?"

"No, Miss Brandy's birthday isn't for several months. These are the children of Titan Mining employees. Mr. Malla always holds a party for them whenever a school trip brings them to Tokra." The chauffeur pointed at one of the men working the grills. "Mr. Malla likes to show his appreciation for the hard work their parents do for the company."

Malla finished flipping a row of burgers, handed his spatula to one of the other men, and walked out to meet Erica and me. Extending his hand, he said, "Jacob Malla."

"Pleased to meet you, Mr. Malla," Erica said for both of us. "I'm Special Agent Erica Hampton of the FBI and this is Captain Nancy Martin."

"Call me Jake." The man turned toward the mansion looming nearby. "I assume you wish to hold our discussion in private?"

"That would be best, sir," Erica said. At Malla's slightly pained expression, she added, "Jake."

We walked in silence for a while, then I asked, "Our driver told us you host a lot of parties like this."

"Yep. These kids spent most of the year living in close quarters with danger lurking all around them. On top of that, they grow up knowing they are just one accident away from being orphaned. I like giving them a chance to blow off steam and have some old-fashioned teenage fun during their visits to Tokra."

"You care about them—and their parents," I said.

"Damned right, I care about them. My employees *are* the company. They work hard for me and I do everything I can to ensure their safety."

A door opened as we approached it. Jake led us inside and down a hallway.

"Or to heal them after an accident." At Jake's terse nod, I said, "You must wish we'd never come here."

"Why? Because it means an end to the supply of body parts I bought for my employees?" I shrugged in response. Jake's eyes smoldered as he motioned us into what was obviously his office. "Bring up that picture you showed Spinnock—the one of those school kids."

I did as instructed, holding my pad up for Jake to see. He tapped a control and a vid image of the pool party popped up on one wall.

The man gave me a top-notch glare, one any drill sergeant would be proud to own. "Do you think I could both host that party and turn a blind eye to what might happen to the children in that picture? I'm a parent, too, and can only imagine how the parents of those missing children must feel. I will do everything in my power to help you rescue those children."

I glanced at Erica, who nodded. Looking back at Jake, I said, "We had to be sure. I hope you understand and are not too offended."

Jake nodded. "I understand. You can't be too careful. Considering that, I'm rather surprised you just walked in here before checking me out."

"Dr. Spinnock's reaction to my revelation and his obvious trust in you spoke volumes," I said.

"Fair enough. What can I do to help you?"

Erica leaned forward, "How did you end up connecting with the people supplying the parts? I mean, spare body parts aren't exactly a readily available commodity."

"For years, I've been trying to connect with hospitals and charitable organizations throughout the frontier, trying to get a line on donated body parts. I offered sizable contributions in return for nothing more than *consideration* when organs and limbs came available. It was all for naught, though, until a man came through here last year. He said he represented a multi-world non-profit which was raising awareness of the medical needs out here on the frontier. For a large donation and reimbursement for the costs of harvesting and delivering organs, he said he could fill our needs."

"I assume you didn't just take him at his word?" Erica asked.

"No, I did not. My legal team investigated his charity and I sent Dr. Spinnock to meet with their specialists. Everything seemed on the level, though it's obvious my lawyers tracked a very clever set of forged documents and Dr. Spinnock was shown a false front." Jake sat back, thinking for a few seconds. "Still, my people were thorough. The level of detail involved in this operation could only be established with some kind of official help."

"You think one of the fringe world governments is behind it?" I asked.

"Probably not an entire government, but at least several high-ranking members of some government."

Erica and I exchanged stunned glances. Our already difficult job had just gotten exponentially harder.

Jake offered us a rueful smile. "I know that's not the news you wanted to hear, but I can't think of any other way those 'charities' could have survived our scrutiny."

Erica nodded, "And wishing otherwise won't get us anywhere. So, who is this guy and where do we find him?"

"His name is Chad Stevens—at least, that's what he was going by a little over a year ago—and his main office was on Ruvis. Since the...goods...are only now arriving, I'm willing to bet he's still operating under that name. The Medical Hope Project, his supposed-charity, still exists and was accepting our donations as recently as three weeks ago."

"Doesn't his location make our lives a lot easier?" I asked. "I mean, he can't quickly warn Miss Perkins or whoever is in charge of things on Osnade. On top of that, any government officials will just be protecting a fake charity, not an organ harvesting operation."

"Yes and no," Erica said. "You're right, the operation on Ruvis is probably just a money laundering scheme, but the officials working with Stevens have to know they're protecting some kind of illegal operation. They may not know what kind of criminals they're working for, but they know they're criminals."

Jake nodded, "Stevens will have very powerful friends in very high places. You won't be able to extradite him—that's assuming the Federation even has an extradition treaty with Ruvis—nor convince any local officials to move against him."

"Wow, you guys had me worried for a minute there," I said, flashing a smile. "I mean, we're not really planning on going through official channels to get this guy, are we?"

"No, we're not," Erica said, "but we'll probably still face some serious challenges because of this man's connections."

I waved a hand dismissively. "Details. And mentioning details, Jake, can you gather everything you have on Stevens and his operation? We're going to need it when we get to Ruvis."

"I already have my people working on that. It's going to take a few hours, though," Jake said. "While we're waiting, could I ask a big favor of you, Captain Martin?"

"Call me Nancy," I said. "If the favor is something within my power, I'll be more than happy to do it."

"I've got three kids from the same family, two sisters and a brother, who lost their father in a decompression accident a few months ago. That's a rare accident around here, thank God, but it means they don't have anyone they can talk to who truly understands what they're going through." Jake looked away, his eyes blinking rapidly for a few seconds. "I can only imagine how painful it must be for you—"

"Of course, I'll talk to those kids," I said. "In all honesty, it'll probably do me as much good as it does them."

"I've got to warn you, they've all been having terrible nightmares about their father," Jake said. "They see—"

"They see him drifting away into the dark void, calling to them," I said, my voice low. "He tells them he's so cold and so lonely and wonders why they've forgotten him."

Jake gave me a startled look, "Uh, yes, that's it, exactly. Are you sure you're up to this, Nancy?"

Drawing a deep breath, I nodded. "It would be best if we did this outside, where it's warm and bright and where we can hear the other kids playing and having fun."

"Do you want me to stay with you, Nancy?" Erica asked. "I lost my husband in an explosion, but it's still the loss of a loved one."

"I appreciate the offer, Erica, but I need to do this on my own. I've lost good friends in explosions, so please don't take this the wrong way, but it's just not the same. I...can't really explain it, but it's not." I turned back to Jake. "Take me to them."

A few minutes later, I watched Jake lead three kids away from the party toward me. I guessed the boy was seventeen and his sisters fifteen and fourteen. The boy walked between his girls, holding their hands. He was doing his best to be the man of the family and obviously found the burden very heavy.

The four of us sat on the grass and talked. I told them about Sko and listened to them talk about their father. The youngest girl was the first to cry and her brother was the last. We cried until we ran out of tears, then we talked and hugged. And sharing the pain lessened it, even for me.

Eventually, Erica signaled that it was time for us to go. I hugged each of the kids one more time and promised to stay in touch with them once our current mission was over. Then, my partner and I flew back to the spaceport and boarded the *Darkheart*.

As we settled into our seats in the pilot's compartment, Erica said, "While you were talking to those kids, I asked Jake if he would mind storing those cargo containers for us. He had people unload everything, so you don't have to worry about balancing the cargo anymore."

"You do know that I mostly did that to aggravate Sam and his crew?"

"Really?" Erica asked, laughing.

"Well, sort of. It's always better to have a balanced load, but I made them 'rebalance' several times after the cargo balance was well within tolerance." I completed my pre-launch check and fired up the engines. "Anyway, I won't miss all that extra mass."

On that note, we lifted off.

Once we were in open space and on course for the wormhole, Erica said, "By my calculations, it'll take us three days to get to Ruvis."

"Two days," I corrected. "We've got plenty of reaction mass and a very powerful engine. I see no reason to lollygag for an extra day when we don't have to. Especially when lives are on the line."

"It's still plenty of time to plan how we should approach this Chad Stevens."

"Erica, should *we* approach him or should *you* approach him? We've got to assume Miss Perkins told Stevens about hiring us to move the cargo. Even if he has no idea who Nancy Martin is, you can bet Perkins filled him in. If I show up at his office, it could ruin our chances of catching him."

"You're probably right, Nancy. I don't see any reason I can't handle the contact. It might be easier with one, anyway."

"Good. Next question—is there any way I can track you if something goes wrong?"

"I was equipped with a standard naval implant when I joined the Fringer Navy. The FBI upgraded a lot of its capabilities when they accepted me, but the basic navy functions are still there, including the emergency beacon. I can just trigger that if I get into trouble."

"Are you willing to give me the codes necessary to turn on the beacon remotely?"

"Like I did when I turned on your implant's sober-up function just before we met?"

"Yes, exactly like that," I growled.

Erica laughed at my expression. "That seems only fair. I *can* count on you to keep a low profile if you need to rescue me?"

"Hey, it's me! Low profile is my middle name."

"Your middle name is Heidi."

"Damn, Erica, is there anything you *don't* know about me?"

"Let me think…" Erica rubbed her chin and gazed thoughtfully out into space. "Um, nope. I'm pretty sure I know everything there is to know about you."

"What's my favorite meal?"

"A cheeseburger with two thin patties, melted cheddar cheese, lettuce, tomato, an onion slice, mustard, mayo, and ketchup. You prefer sesame seed buns but can live without them. You like following that with a thick slice of chocolate cake." Erica glanced over at me. "Wait, I just realized there *is* something I don't know about you."

"And what, pray tell, do you not know?"

"Why that kind of food doesn't go straight to your hips."

Erica dissolved into a giggling fit. I punched her in the arm, which only made her giggle harder. She was still at it when we entered the wormhole.

# CHAPTER FIVE

I didn't quite make the Ruvis run in two days, but that's only because we ran into traffic approaching the planet. To my surprise, Ruvis had a population on par with a medium-sized Federation world. People from the Federation generally assume frontier worlds are sparsely populated and we're usually right, but Ruvis had nearly two billion people living on it.

Eying the number of ships queued up for landing, I said, "I guess this rules out us swooping down on Stevens, grabbing him, and making a run for the wormhole."

"That was never part of our plan, Nancy."

"Maybe not, but I bet it would be a lot more fun than our actual plan."

Knowing I wasn't serious, Erica ignored my comment. "My request for a docking bay in the city of Vuenaas was approved. That puts us into landing queue six with four ships ahead of us."

"I assume Vuenaas is where Stevens has his offices?"

"Yep. I've also called the office with a request for an appointment with Mr. Stevens. With any luck, Jake's letter of introduction will help with that."

"Do you think Stevens will buy the former-employee-forming-her-own-company line from Jake?" I asked.

"I don't see why not. From our brief conversations with Jake, it strikes me as exactly the sort of thing he'd do," Erica replied. "And it's not like we're setting up business in the same system, so we won't be in direct competition with Titan Mining."

"You *do* remember that we're not setting up a mining company at all, right?"

Erica turned a haughty expression on me. "I'm a *method* agent, Nancy, so I will thank you not to interfere with my immersion in the role."

I rolled my eyes and sighed theatrically. "Yes, ma'am. Please remind me of the name you're immersing yourself in."

"Amaya Yumisa, CEO of Astral Mining Company."

"And have you figured out where we'll be doing all that mining?"

Erica gave a brief, unamused smile. "I'm sorry, we're keeping that information secret at this time. Claim jumpers, you know."

"What's the name of the company ship that brought you here?"

"Unless you screwed up changing our ID in the transponder, this is the *Deep Venture* piloted by Amy Zarn."

"I think you'll do just fine," I said. "Are you sure your listening device will escape detection if Stevens decides to be paranoid and scan you?"

"It's the latest tech from the FBI labs. Nothing against Ruvis, but I seriously doubt they have any scanners that can find it."

We waited in the landing queue for another forty-six minutes before receiving clearance. I brought us down nice and easy, settling into our docking bay in Vuenaas without raising even a cloud of dust, much less any suspicions. I arranged for refueling and then Erica and I headed out for a late lunch. Midway through the meal, Erica received confirmation of an appointment with Chad Stevens.

Erica's eyebrows rose as she read the message. "It seems Mr. Stevens is tied up during office hours but wonders if Ms. Yumisa would join him for a business dinner at his favorite restaurant."

"Business dinner my ass," I said.

"You don't think he'll discuss business with me?" Erica asked.

"Yeah, I'm sure he'll start off discussing business. Then he'll suggest you continue the discussion over drinks at his place. Before you know it, he'll be doing his best to talk you right out of your clothes and into his bed."

"The man hasn't met me nor seen me. What makes you think he'll go straight for seduction?"

"You placed a vid call to his office, right?" Erica nodded, so I continued, "And you talked to a real person?"

"A female receptionist, yes. But she's the only one I spoke with."

"She, knowing her boss, will no doubt include 'smoking hot' in her report to Stevens."

"Smoking hot? Where do you get these things, Nancy?"

"Next time you're looking in a mirror, Erica, try looking at yourself the way a guy would. You're the type of woman who makes old geezers wish they were eighty years younger."

"Let's assume you're right—"

"I am."

"*Anyway*, it might give me a chance to pump Stevens for more information. If I appear receptive to his advances but insist on putting business before pleasure..."

I nodded thoughtfully. "That could work. Of course, you're going to have to dress the part, too. Have you got anything that's too sexy for regular business wear but not entirely inappropriate for business dinner meeting?"

Erica gave me a confused look. "You lost me with that one."

"I'll take that as a 'no' then." I checked my chrono. "Finish eating quickly. We've got shopping to do."

It took me less time to find the right dress for Erica than it did to convince her to wear it.

"Look at how short it is! How will I sit down in this without flashing Stevens?"

I grinned at her. "You probably won't. That's why I selected underwear that's essentially the same color as your skin. Stevens will be so preoccupied trying to figure out if you're wearing anything under the dress that he'll be permanently distracted."

"Oh, that makes me feel *much* better."

"Just try it on, okay?" I asked.

Erica glared at me, took the clothes, and marched to the dressing room muttering, "It's for the children. It's for the children."

When she viewed herself in the dress, she was both appalled and astounded—appalled at just how short the dress was and astounded at just how good she looked in it.

"I don't know, Nancy, it just shows so much of...everything."

"And everything it shows looks great." I put on a serious expression for a minute. "You said it yourself going to the dressing room—it's for the children. Children who may not have time for you to be modest."

Erica gave me a pained expression. "That's easy for you to say. You're not the one wearing the dress."

"No, but I would in a heartbeat if it would help those kids."

Erica closed her eyes and sighed, "You're right. Let's buy it."

Much to my partner's disgust, I made her practice wearing the dress the rest of the afternoon. It took her a while, but she finally figured out how to sit down without flashing the whole room while also giving someone seated across from her the briefest of glimpses of what I insisted on calling 'the promised land.' When the time came for her to leave, even Erica felt confident wearing the outfit.

I listened in over dinner and had no trouble hearing the lust in Stevens' otherwise cultured and controlled voice. The first time he tried steering the conversation away from business, Erica was ready for him.

"I *always* put business before pleasure, Chad," she purred. "I just *hate* it when some undiscussed business item rises up and interferes with my fun."

"Ah, so you like to commit your mind and body to the task at hand?" Stevens asked.

"Mm hm. Besides, the anticipation adds some interesting spice to negotiations, don't you think?"

Damn, the girl was good! I could imagine Stevens literally drooling at the mouth right about now. Apparently, I was right about him. He rushed through negotiations with hardly any actual negotiating. He was finally rewarded with the words he most wanted to hear.

"That covers all of my business questions," Erica said. "Do you have any for me?"

"One or two, but why don't we go back to my place first. I'll ask them over drinks."

A couple of minutes later, they were on their way to Stevens' apartment. They kept to inane small talk during the ride. Once there, Erica 'freshened up' while Stevens prepared the drinks. My partner took advantage of the brief moment of privacy to assure me all was going according to plan.

"My implant is running the anti-intoxication program. All I have to do is make Stevens match me drink for drink. Once he's drunk, we move on to the next step in the plan."

After that hastily whispered bit of encouraging news, Erica returned to her host. I heard glasses clink followed by the subtle sounds of drinking. Then Stevens took the glasses for a refill. So far, so good.

Returning with refilled drinks, Stevens asked, "Are you ready to answer my questions?"

"Sshhure...am," Erica said.

Where the hell did that slur in her voice come from? That was very definitely *not* part of the plan—at least not this early. I felt the first pangs of alarm ringing in my head.

"That's good," Stevens said. "Why don't you sit down and get comfortable? This won't take very long and you won't remember a thing."

Damn, damn, and damn! The bastard must have dosed Erica with some kind of truth drug.

Through the listening device, I heard Stevens say, "Tell me about the Astral Mining Company."

Erica giggled. "Ish not real. Fffooled you, din' it?"

Stevens sighed, "Are you bugged?"

"You betcha, baby!"

"Turn it off."

All sound immediately cut off.

Dammit, why hadn't Erica or I considered the possibility Stevens would drug her? It's not like this operation had run so smoothly that we should have gotten complacent. I shoved recriminations from my mind as I keyed in the code for the emergency beacon in Erica's implant. Seconds later, I was rewarded with a pulsing dot on the ship's scanners. At least the dot was green, showing Erica was alive and in good health for the moment.

I overlaid a map of the city on the scanner screen. Stevens' apartment was northwest of our docking bay, on the edge of the city. I could be there in a matter of minutes in a flitter if only I had one. That made *two* things we hadn't planned for. God, Erica and I spent way too much time planning how she was going to seduce Stevens and way too little planning for what could go wrong. Renting a flitter, or even a ground car, as an off-worlder would take me thirty minutes if I was very lucky. An hour was more like it, and that was assuming no one else was there ahead of me. I didn't want to take a taxi, but it wasn't like I had any other choices.

I was on the comm calling for the cab when Erica's beacon began moving. The blinking dot moved out at surprising speed, meaning she was in a vehicle of some kind. Worse, it was headed further northwest—out of the city. Indecision gripped me for a few seconds as I tried to come up with a reasonable way to chase my partner. The robotic taxi dispatcher queried several times as my mind raced through my options. I realized, with both relief and trepidation, that I only had one way to get to my partner.

"Never mind," I said into the comm and disconnected.

Then I began the emergency startup procedure for the *Darkheart's* engines.

Once again, I felt grateful for the foresight of the FBI design team. Like military engines' tolerance for extreme thrust changes, they also have a specialized, extremely fast emergency startup procedure. A combat ship with no power is useless in the case of a surprise attack, so the military requires a maximum startup time of sixty seconds. The *Darkheart's* Nexus class engine only takes forty-three seconds to reach full power.

As the engine came on, a woman's voice issued from the comm. "*Deep Venture*, this is Vuenaas Control. Respond."

It took a second for me to remember that was the name broadcast by our transponder. I keyed on the comm and said, "This is *Deep Venture*. I'm a little busy here, so make this quick."

"Your engine is going through an emergency startup."

"Tell me something I don't know, Control."

"You do not have clearance to lift off. Please shutdown your engine."

Time to find out just how well Control listens. "This is an emergency situation and beyond my control."

"Say again, *Deep Venture*?"

"I am facing a serious emergency, Control. Shutting down could result in the loss of life," I said, hoping Control would infer what I wanted rather than hear what I said.

"Are you requesting an emergency liftoff clearance, *Deep Venture*?"

Ha! Control took the bait. Putting all of the sarcasm I could muster into my voice, I said, "Gee, Control. I don't know. Do you think I need that?" I paused for a second and then yelled, "Of course I'm requesting emergency clearance—and you'd better grant it in the next ten seconds!"

"Understood. Clearance granted." A red emergency light began flashing on my scanner screen and a no-fly zone appeared centered on my docking bay. "Head straight for orbit, *Deep Venture*. Emergency response teams will rendezvous with you there and render all assistance possible."

"Thank you, Control. *Deep Venture* lifting off now."

Inwardly wincing at the damage I was about to do to the docking bay, I threw emergency lift-off power to the engines. My ship shot up into the night sky above Vuenaas, gaining altitude quickly. Once I was above the standard traffic levels, I swung the ship's nose around and raced northwest.

Erica's green dot was still on the screen, but it was moving extremely fast and not sticking to the roads. Obviously, Stevens had a flitter, and a high-end one, at that. Realizing that did make me stop berating myself for not having gotten one of our own earlier. It was still a horrible oversight on our part, but chances are I'd never have been able to keep up with Stevens' flitter in a rental. The *Darkheart* was a different matter.

"*Deep Venture*, why have you veered off course?"

"It's because of that emergency situation, Control. I have no choice over the ship's flight path." I took a moment to twitch the controls in a few random directions, gasping and swearing as if I was fighting hard to maintain some form of level flight. "Control, I request you enforce a wide no-fly zone along my current course while I deal with this emergency."

In response, a cone formed in front of my ship's icon on the scanner screen. Flitter traffic ahead of me veered off to one side or landed. I kept my eye on Erica's blinking icon and realized it was increasing speed. Stevens must have a top-of-the-line flitter because the thing was really hauling ass in front of me. Why didn't he simply land or move out of the way, like other flitters? Vuenaas Control didn't include my ship's name in the emergency broadcast, so Stevens had no reason for concern.

I felt the hairs on the back of my neck stand up when I figured it out. Stevens sped up because he wasn't far from his destination. On top of that, he could do whatever he was going to do to Erica with the certainty that all official eyes were on the runaway spaceship. It gave him a tailor-made distraction. I could imagine the man almost cackling with glee at the way events were falling into place for him. I could also imagine him having time to kill Erica before I reached them.

I'd kept the throttle at half-power to keep atmospheric friction heat from building up and damaging the hull. So far, the FBI shipbuilders had given me full military-level equipment. Praying their thoroughness extended to the hull, I increased to full throttle while twitching the *Darkheart's* controls some more.

"*Deep Venture*, throttle back before your hull overheats and you crash!"

"No can do, Control. I'm still facing a possible loss of life if I do that."

Control was quiet for just a tad too long. When she spoke again, suspicion tinged Control's voice. "*Deep Venture*, what is the exact nature of your emergency?"

Well, I got more time out of my bluff than I had any right to expect. Still, maybe I could get one more concession from Control before my bluff fell apart. I was gaining rapidly on Stevens' flitter. Time to see if I could get the guy to land.

Ignoring Control's question, I said, "My scans show a flitter dead ahead. It looks like the pilot is trying to outrun me, which is damned stupid considering how fast I'm going. Control, can you please order him to land?"

"You could just throttle down and return to your docking bay, *Deep Venture*."

"No, I couldn't. I really do have an emergency situation and it really will result in the loss of life, *not* including the guy flying that flitter, if I don't respond to it."

"We have him on our screens, too, *Deep Venture*. I've got a traffic control supervisor calling him now. Rest assured, this interference with Vuenaas traffic will be one of *many* charges filed against you unless you have a very good explanation for this behavior."

"If traffic charges are the worst thing I face after this is over, I'll gladly pay any fine and serve whatever time is required, Control."

"You could try explaining your emergency, *Deep Venture*," Control said, a bit of uncertainty replacing the suspicion in her voice. "If you really are facing a life or death situation we are more than ready to help as best we can."

Ahead of me, Stevens' flitter, with Erica's beacon still flashing green, began descending. Its speed dropped, too. Shortly, the flitter dropped low enough to vanish from my screens, but the green dot from Erica's beacon kept blinking. A few seconds after my scanner lost track of the flitter, the blinking green dot accelerated down one of the roads. The bastard just waited until he was off Control's screens to resume his run. Following the road forced him to keep his speed down, at least.

As I roared over Stevens' head, I caught sight of a large lake ahead. A quick check of the map on my scanner showed the road Stevens was following crossed the water at one of the lake's narrower stretches. Seeing the bridge gave me a very bad feeling. Could Stevens be planning on dumping my drugged partner into the lake and leaving her to drown?

Looking at the lake and bridge, I imagined Stevens' changing from his original plan, whatever that was, to a much simpler one. With all traffic grounded, Stevens wouldn't have to worry about prying eyes as he flew his flitter out over the lake. Then he could just push Erica out of the door—or, since the drug had her in a suggestible state, tell her to get out. Too drugged to swim, Erica would drown in the lake while Stevens zipped back to the location where Vuenaas Control told him to land.

I could file a complaint with the police, of course, but it wouldn't do any good. After all, it would be the word of his victim's pilot against the word of a man with significant connections with Ruvis's politicians. Even if I came completely clean, admitting to the FBI connection, the listening device, and everything, it's unlikely Stevens would face more than a few questions from the police.

Yes, Stevens had plenty of reasons to feel confident. But there was one extremely big reason he should worry, and I was piloting it. Only, Stevens hadn't a clue I was the reason he'd been ordered to land.

"Control, I think I'm going to take you up on the offer and bring the *Deep Venture* down in the lake just ahead of me."

"Roger that, *Deep Venture*. Emergency personnel are en route. Can you tell me whether this is a medical or law enforcement emergency?"

"Yes," I replied.

"Which, *Deep Venture*? Or do you mean both?"

"Both. Got to go silent now, Control, and concentrate on putting this thing down."

"I'm alerting police and medical personnel, now. Soft landings, *Deep Venture*."

Putting aside the question of dealing with first responders, I concentrated on pulling off my hastily formed rescue plan. I brought the ship down until it was flying just above the trees surrounding the lake. Keeping one eye on the blinking green dot representing Erica, I deployed the forward laser battery and throttled back to half speed. I thought I'd have perhaps ten seconds from the time I was over the lake to get the ship into position to pull off my plan.

The ship flashed over the lake's shore and I engaged just about every thruster available. The ship bucked as maneuvering thrusters pivoted the ship in midair. When the nose was facing the bridge, I pushed the throttle to the maximum just long enough to bring the ship to a stop. Steam rose all around me as the thrusters instantly boiled the lake water beneath me. I ignored it all and grabbed the targeting controls for the laser battery. With a few quick movements, I brought the battery to bear on the bridge.

The flitter zipped out of the trees, hugging the road. I could only imagine Stevens' expression when he saw the front end of the *Darkheart* sticking out of the gathering steam, but the flitter never wobbled once. Thanking God I'd spent my navy career flying starfighters, where I'd become a damned good shot with a ship's laser. I targeted the flitter's engine compartment and fired.

A bright beam of coherent light lanced through the steam cloud and slagged the flitter's engine. Its lift completely gone, the little craft dropped a meter to the road below it. I was already moving the *Darkheart* as the flitter, skidding along on its undercarriage, bounced off the guardrail on the right side of the bridge. As I swung my ship around and over the bridge, the flitter bounced back and forth from guardrail to guardrail, no doubt jarring the passengers, but also reducing speed quickly.

When the flitter slid to a stop, I offered up a quick prayer that the bridge could hold the weight of the *Darkheart* and set her down five meters behind what was left of an extremely expensive vehicle. I was sliding through the pilot's compartment emergency exit before the ship fully settled onto its landing struts. Behind me, I heard the comm spring to life as Vuenaas Control tried to find out what was going on.

Making sure my blaster was set to stun, I sprinted toward the downed flitter. I hadn't taken two steps when the back left door flew open. A muscular man staggered out of the craft, a large blaster gripped in one hand. He had some trouble focusing on me, but that didn't slow down his reflexes. His blaster swung toward me with startling speed. Unprepared for the man's quickness, I dove to the ground. As a deadly blaster bolt burned through the air over my head, I snapped off three shots at the man. My first shot went wide, but the man jerked as the second and third shots hit him in the center of his considerable mass.

I rolled back to my feet and covered the last few meters to the flitter. A handsome, dapper man—Stevens, no doubt—

fought to open the driver's door. Erica was curled up on the floor in the backseat. Her short skirt was bunched up around her waist, but that could have happened while the flitter caromed back and forth between the guardrails. Other than that, she looked like she was sleeping.

Placing my blaster against Stevens' head, I said, "Forget the door. I want you to climb into the backseat and gently carry my boss out of this flitter. Do you understand?"

Stevens went still at the touch of the blaster. Nodding his head, he began squirming his way between the two front seats. "You won't get away with this, you know. I have friends in very high places."

"Yeah, I know all about your powerful pals and I don't give a damn about them," I snarled. Aware I couldn't have more than a minute or two before the emergency vehicles got here, I added, "Move faster or I'll stun your ass and drag you out feet first."

Stevens picked up the pace and was standing next to me with Erica in his arms fifteen seconds later. "What are you going to do to me?"

"I just want you to carry my boss onto the ship. After that, you can go wherever you want."

Stevens turned and stumbled toward the *Darkheart*. "I don't know how much this woman is paying you, but I'll double it. I can use talented people like you."

"Not interested."

"I see you're loyal, too." Stevens' voice held tones of warm approval. "But even loyal people have a price. What if I quadruple whatever this woman is paying you."

Stevens stopped next to the ship while I coded open the hatch. I listened hard for approaching sirens and thought I heard several. Stevens must still be too shaken up by the wreck to hear the sirens yet. The hatch slid open and I motioned for him to go inside.

Playing for time, I asked, "If I say yes, how are you going to make this whole incident disappear?"

Stevens flashed a big, though somewhat bloody, smile at me. "Does it really matter *how* I do it, as long as I *can* do it?"

We entered the living area and the man dropped Erica onto one of the couches.

Stevens turned to me, one of his hands extended. "So, have we got a deal?"

"No," I said, shutting the hatch. "And I lied about letting you go after you carried her onto the ship."

Stevens' eyes were just widening when I shot him.

Time was short and I needed to get my butt into the pilot's seat fast. I also knew I might need Erica's help getting away. Without a second thought, I grabbed the med kit mounted on the bulkhead and flipped it open. I slapped the unit against my partner's upper arm.

"Med unit, she has been drugged. Identify the drug and neutralize it."

I turned and ran for the pilot's compartment, not bothering to wait for an acknowledgment. Sliding into my seat, I began fastening the harness. My eyes darted to the scanner, which showed the closest emergency vehicle was less than a kilometer from me. If I didn't get off the ground immediately, I could easily find myself choosing between capture and ramming the first responders.

"Autopilot, emergency take off *now*."

The way-too-calm voice of the autopilot said, "I cannot comply. A no-fly zone exists above us."

Still working on my harness, I said, "Emergency override omega three seven zero sigma."

"Emergency override accepted."

The *Darkheart's* engine roared and she rose quickly into the night sky. It was only then that I realized Vuenaas Control was still blathering over the comm. I ignored it long enough to check the scanner. The nearest emergency flitter was so close it was tossed around in the *Darkheart's* atmospheric wake like a toy. Just when I feared I'd knocked the craft out of the sky, its pilot regained control and landed on the bridge I'd just left.

Keying the comm, I said, "Control, this is the *Deep Venture*. I was unable to complete a landing, but now have the ship heading for orbit."

"*Deep Venture*, you will land your ship immediately and surrender to the authorities currently onsite. Is that clear?"

"I can't do that, Control. I'm still dealing with that life or death situation."

"*Deep Venture*, we both know there is no emergency. You have been lying to me ever since you started your engines."

"Incorrect, Control. I have been entirely truthful to you throughout this incident."

"You expect me to believe that after you shot down a civilian flitter?"

"I don't know what you're talking about, Control."

"Drop the act, *Deep Venture*. You nearly knocked a pair of police officers out of the air. Did you really think they wouldn't report the wrecked flitter on that bridge or notice the laser damage to it? Did you think our scanners wouldn't pick up your weapons discharge? I repeat, land *now* or we will be forced to take more drastic measures."

With my harness finally fastened, I said, "Pilot is assuming manual control."

"Manual control acknowledged," the autopilot responded and released the controls to me.

I swung the bow of the ship straight up, maximizing the *Darkheart's* aerodynamics. A quick check of our altitude showed we were high enough that our exhaust wouldn't affect the people on the ground, so I gave the engines full throttle once again. The ship vibrated as it rammed its way through the atmosphere. It took all of my concentration to keep the ship pointed straight up, as high-altitude winds and pockets of turbulence tried to knock us off course.

"*Deep Venture*, you are making a very big mistake. I implore you—"

"Control, I assume you don't want this ship crashing into the ground, so shut up and let me concentrate on piloting her safely into orbit."

To my surprise, Control did as I requested. The comm remained silent as I fought the controls and guided the *Darkheart* through the atmosphere and into space. Of course, Control was back the moment I cleared atmo.

"*Deep Venture*, you are out of my zone. If you have any sense of self-preservation, you will listen carefully to the next voice you hear and follow his instructions to the letter. Vuenaas Control out."

A no-nonsense male voice immediately replaced the woman's voice. "*Deep Venture*, this is Ruvis Space Control. Cut your main engine and maneuver into a parking orbit immediately. This station's laser batteries are targeting you as I speak. If you do not comply, we will open fire on you."

Unsteady footsteps sounded behind me. Erica staggered into the compartment and plopped into her seat. The med unit was still attached to her arm, the active light blinking away as it worked to completely scrub the drug from her system. At least it had already cleared enough that my partner was more or less functional again.

Gazing out into space, Erica said, "How long have I been out and what have I missed?"

"Less than an hour and one hell of a lot," I said. "I'll fill in the details later. Right now, can you to find me the closest concentration of civilian ships? I need the course five minutes ago."

As Erica bent over her console, I said into the comm, "You don't want to fire on this ship, Control."

"You are quite correct, *Deep Venture*, but I will give the order if you do not comply."

"We have Ruvis citizen Chad Stevens on board, Control. Perhaps you should run that name up the chain of command before you do something you'll regret for the rest of your extremely short career."

In the silence which followed my announcement, Erica said, "Course two eight one by one six will take us right through the heart of the Ruvis landing queues."

I put the ship on the new heading. "We'll be among the queues for approaching ships in fifty-six seconds, Erica. Can you find a comm channel all ships will hear?"

"Already got it, Nancy. You can broadcast on the Ruvis emergency channel." The med unit's detoxification procedure must have been nearly complete because my partner turned one of her more devilish smiles my way. "That channel is reserved for official use only. You could get into big trouble if you use it without authorization."

"No problem—you're the one who's going to use it. On my mark, broadcast a warning to all ships to maintain their exact course regardless of what is going on around them. Any ship that breaks from its course may endanger itself and us. We will fire upon any such ship."

"Are we really going to fire on innocent ships, Nancy?" Erica asked.

"Only if it's a choice between them or us." I locked eyes with her for a brief second. "Remember how many kids will die if we fail, Erica."

She nodded unhappily and deployed all of our weapons.

"*Deep Venture*, put Mr. Stevens on the comm so he can explain this situation."

"I wish I could, Control, but he's not feeling very talkative at the moment."

"In other words, you have kidnapped him."

"I prefer thinking of it as an arrest, Control."

"Do you have any legal authority to make arrests on Ruvis, *Deep Venture*?"

"It's a citizen's arrest, Control."

"You're not a citizen of Ruvis. Only citizens can make a *citizen's* arrest."

"Broadcast in five seconds, Erica."

A laser blast flashed by outside the ship—a miss, but a damned close one.

"As you can see, we once again have authorization to fire. You cannot hope to evade all of the base's laser batteries. Surrender *now*."

"Erica, *go!*" As my partner began broadcasting, I once again turned my attention to the comm. "Control, I believe you've been too distracted checking into our unwilling passenger and getting the okay to shoot at us to have analyzed our course. Before firing again, I strongly suggest you do that."

The comm fell silent once again while Erica continued repeating her broadcast. Anticipating the station would take one more shot at us before we got in among the civilian traffic, I reversed all thrust. With the inertial dampeners engaged, neither Erica or I felt anything. But we both saw two laser shots blaze by directly ahead of us.

I reversed thrust a second time and we were once again driving toward the approach queues. Grinning at my own brilliance, I said, "I bet Space Control didn't know our ship could pull off that maneuver."

Then we were among the other ships, making it far too risky for Space Control to try another shot.

"Ha! By the time we're clear of these approach queues, we'll be outside of the effective range of the station-based laser batteries."

Erica frowned and said, "That's strange. Space Control is now broadcasting the same basic message I was, except they're promising stiff fines for ships that disobey."

"They don't want anything to happen to these ships. Trade is the lifeblood of any planet with a decent-sized population." Handing Erica my blaster, I added, "Why don't you go secure Stevens. He should be out for a while longer, but there's no sense taking any chances. You should search him, while you're at it."

"You can handle things up here on your own?" she asked.

"I'll be fine for a couple of minutes," I replied. "Just don't dawdle."

"Roger that, Captain Martin," Erica said, heading aft.

She hadn't been gone more than ten seconds when the scanner picked up a dozen new signals leaving the space station. I had a good guess what I was seeing, but waited for the scanner to provide more details. They weren't long in coming.

Ruvis Space Control had just launched a squadron of starfighters.

# CHAPTER SIX

The twelve dots representing the starfighters gained speed far faster than I'd have preferred. Like me, the pilots were running their engines at maximum thrust. The only problem was that the starfighters had a much better thrust-to-mass ratio. Over the long haul, my greater thrust could overcome the *Darkheart's* considerable mass and pull away from the fighters. In the short run—such as our current flight to the wormhole—the smaller ships would be within firing range of us for at least ten minutes.

To a civilian, ten minutes might not sound like a very long time. In combat, ten minutes is like a lifetime. Many times, it *is* a lifetime—or the end of a lifetime, anyway. My eyes ran over the console, looking for some inspiration from the lesser-used controls. If this was an adventure vid, I'd spot some obscure button and exclaim, "Of course! I can cross the technobabble flow with the negative current whatchamacallit. That will double our thrust if the engine doesn't immediately explode. But, by God, that's a risk I'm willing to take!"

Have you ever noticed that adventure vid heroes never run their dangerous ideas past the people who will be killed if the idea fails? It never dawned on me before this. Why I thought of it now, in the middle of a real life-and-death situation, is beyond me. I guess it's one of the mysteries of the human mind.

Pushing all of that speculation aside, I called, "Erica? I could use your help up here right now."

I heard the slap of bare feet running up the corridor. My partner must have removed the high heels she wore on her 'date' with our unwilling passenger.

"What's the situation, Nancy?" she asked, sliding into her seat and immediately getting to work fastening her harness.

I waved a hand at the scanner screen. "Ruvis Space Control launched a squadron of starfighters when we flew in among the civilian ships."

Erica studied the screen for several seconds and then said, "I assume we're going as fast as we can?"

"Yes."

"Those fighters are going to be in firing range for a damned long time."

"Tell me something I don't know."

"When the time comes, I can run all of our shield power to the aft generators. That will buy us some extra time. How much depends on the pilots' accuracy."

"Assume they're going to hit us a lot, Erica. Fighter pilots train to shoot at much smaller, much more agile targets—other starfighters. In comparison, hitting the *Darkheart* will only be slightly more challenging than hitting the space station the fighters launched from."

"Gee, you know how to build a girl's confidence, Nancy." Erica studied the scanner a bit more and then got a thoughtful expression. "Since we can't speed up, what if I can get the fighters to slow down?"

"By all means, go for it."

"You're not going to like part of my plan," my partner added.

"Will I dislike it more than I dislike the idea of those kids getting cut up for parts?"

"Absolutely not."

"Then your plan has my blessing."

Erica grabbed the comm, which was still set to the emergency channel. Someone from Space Control continued broadcasting the warning to the ships around us, ordering them to maintain their current course.

"To all civilian ships in queues four, five, and six. This is the *Deep Venture*, originator of the order to maintain your course." Erica glanced at the scanner screen again, as if confirming something, and then said, "You are ordered to come to course one oh one by two six four. We will fire on you if you do not comply."

Space Control immediately said, "All ships, ignore that order and maintain your current course. That is a direct order from Ruvis Space Control."

"That's easy for Space Control to say since they aren't the ones facing a heavily armed ship," Erica countered. "I repeat, all ships come around to course one oh one by two six four. You have five seconds before we open fire."

A few smaller ships peeled away and followed Erica's order, but the larger ships maintained their original courses. Watching the small ships, I understood my partner's plan. The new course carried those ships right into the path of the oncoming starfighters. No matter how the fighters dealt with the ships, it would slow down their pursuit. But that would only happen if enough ships changed course, and that wasn't happening.

"Nice try, Erica," I said.

"Don't give up yet, Nancy," she replied.

Pulling up the weapons console, Erica's fingers flew over the controls and laser beams lanced from the *Darkheart*. One shot scorched the side of a huge, lumbering cargo ship. Another slagged the aft scanner array for a large spaceliner. A third seared the space just ahead of an ore hauler. The remaining shots flew off into space, not coming near any ships.

Keying the comm again, Erica said, "All ships, those were warning shots. I got two hits and the intentional near-miss to prove I know what I'm doing. The other five shots were a show of force. I was a capital ship gunnery officer during the Federation-Fringer war a few years ago. If you do not follow my orders, my next nine shots will all have targets. Acknowledge by coming around to course one oh one by two six four."

The scanner showed the ships in the three queues named by Erica rotating onto her dictated course. With ships ranging in size from tiny space yachts to bulky cargo ships, it was a very ragged course change. But it *was* a course change for all of the ships.

Space Control wasn't willing to give up that easily. "All ships in queues four through six, return to your original courses. That is an order! If you fail to comply, you will face stiff fines and may have your cargo confiscated. Repeating, all ships in queues four through six, resume your original course."

Just in case some of the ships were reconsidering their course change, Erica said, "Any ship returning to their original course will be fired upon with all available laser batteries. I'd choose the stiff fine if I were you. Besides, do you really think Ruvis Space Control is going to fine you for protecting yourself from an armed vessel rampaging through your midst? That's bad for business."

To emphasize her words, Erica sent another spray of laser fire flashing through the ships. None of the shots hit, but most of them were very close misses.

"To all civilian ships," she broadcast after firing, "that is the last time I will purposefully miss. We have no desire to harm any of you, but our mission is life-and-death—and not *our* lives or deaths. We will succeed or die in the attempt. Try to thwart us and I promise you will die before we do."

Ruvis Space Control raved and raged at the ships converging on the starfighters' course, but he didn't back up his words with laser beams. The ships did not turn aside. The fighters had little choice but to decrease thrust and fly around the mass of ships. Unsurprisingly, the ships in queues one, two, and three also broke from their orderly lines and took the most direct course away from the *Darkheart*.

With the approach lanes clear, I adjusted our own course, putting us on a straight line shot at the wormhole. Meanwhile, Erica studied the scanner screen for nearly a full minute while simultaneously making calculations on her console. When she looked up, her face wore a self-satisfied smile.

"By my calculations, the closest of the starfighters can have us in firing range for a maximum of ten seconds. If they stay on that course long enough to take the shot, they may get too close to the wormhole and get dragged in after us."

Wincing at the thought of any ships without inertial dampeners getting sucked into a wormhole, I said, "Would you please broadcast that to the pursuing starfighters. I'm sure they can—and will—run the numbers, but we might as well get them thinking about it immediately."

Erica did as I asked. I don't know whether the space station or the fighter pilots plotted the time to firing range calculations, but three minutes after Erica's final broadcast, the fighters broke off their pursuit. Heaving a sigh of relief, I throttled back to allow for better control as we approached the wormhole. Thirteen and a half minutes later, the gray fog of the wormhole engulfed us. We'd made our escape from Ruvis.

As Ruvis vanished from our scanners, I glanced at Erica. "I think it's time we had a talk with our guest. I don't suppose he kept a vial of the drug he put in your drink?"

"Not that I could find," she said. "I wouldn't count on appealing to his good nature, either."

I finished unfastening my harness and stood up. "That thought never crossed my mind."

In the living area, I found Stevens manacled to the table. He was bent over it with his head rocking back and forth as consciousness returned. Unfocused eyes turned my way, but the man wasn't fully awake yet.

I grabbed the med unit and slapped it on his arm. "Med unit, this man was stunned by a blaster. Help him recover quickly."

The unit beeped acknowledgment and started doing whatever it is med units do in this situation.

"Have you got a plan?" Erica asked. "If not, all I ask for is a cutting laser. I guarantee I'll get him to talk."

"I have no doubt you will, Erica, but let's save that for the last resort. In the long run, that kind of thing will probably harm you worse than it hurts Stevens."

My partner shrugged. "I think I can live with anything I have to do if it gets those children home safely."

"Maybe," I said, watching Stevens' eyes blink rapidly as they tried to focus on Erica and me, "but let me try my idea, first."

"What does your idea involve?"

"It starts by stripping Stevens naked and then dragging him into the closest airlock."

"I don't know, Nancy. Throwing someone out of an airlock only works if there's a second thug who becomes real talkative after watching his buddy get sucked into space."

"That's not my plan, Erica. At least, it's not the only part of my plan. I'm going to need a couple of EVA harnesses, too."

Erica's eyebrows arched in surprise but Stevens spoke before she could ask for more details.

"You two bitches have no idea how much trouble you're in."

The man's slurred voice robbed the threat of any real potency, but he did manage a good glare to go along with it. Erica and I ruined the moment by laughing at him.

Erica bent over and looked him in the eye. "Exactly who do you think is going to make good on your threat, Chad? No one knows who we are."

"How stupid do you think the authorities are on Ruvis? They won't have any trouble tying my wrecked flitter to this 'runaway' ship," Stevens said. "Messenger drones are probably already heading for every wormhole out of Ruvis with your names, descriptions, and your ship registration information."

"The descriptions could be a minor problem," Erica admitted, "but everything else you think you know about us is fiction."

Stevens shook his head vigorously. "No way. My staff checked your credentials and ship information thoroughly. It's all legit—not a forgery among them."

My partner leaned closer to Stevens and whispered, "I'm going to tell you a little secret, Stevens. The Terran Federation has at least half-a-dozen agencies that create legitimate though false identities for people and ships, throughout the fringe worlds, the rim worlds, and even out here on the frontier worlds. So, yes, our identities are both legit *and* false." Erica sat back and grinned at Stevens. "That's pretty neat, huh?"

Uncertainty crept into Stevens' eyes. "My associates will still find you and make you pay."

Erica stood up. "Are you trying to convince us or yourself?"

I pulled out a vibroblade and began slicing the clothes off of Stevens. "I think that's enough chitchat. It's time for Mr. Stevens to answer our questions."

"Not that I'm going to tell you anything, but what do you want to know?" Stevens asked.

I stopped cutting clothes long enough to say, "Where is the organ harvesting facility used by Miss Perkins' group? Are the young people she'll kill for their organs kept there? What kind of defenses will we face? What kind of protection arrangements do they have with the planetary government?"

Stevens stared at me and then began laughing. "Two of you against Perkins and her people? After they capture you, I'm going to make sure they harvest your organs while you're awake and aware of the procedures. And I'm going to enjoy every last—"

Erica punched Stevens in the nose. Turning away from the blood pouring down the man's face, she said quietly, "He's right about the numbers, at least. We'll be horribly outnumbered and, if we find the kids—"

"*When* we find the kids," I interrupted.

"Right. When we find the kids, how can the two of us hope to get them all moving together?"

"I've got a couple of ideas about that. Once I get started interrogating our guest, I'll need you to program some messenger drones of our own. We'll launch them as soon as we exit the wormhole."

"It would help if you told me what the messages were and who they're for, Nancy."

"Not while our pal Chad can hear. I doubt he'll get away from us, but I'm not willing to take the risk when it's so easy to avoid." I pulled out my blaster, setting it to the lowest power stun setting available. "Okay, Erica, remove his manacles. And Stevens, don't get any bright ideas. I'll stun you as many times as necessary. And if you make me stun you too many times, I'll also cut off your favorite bit of anatomy. Is that clear?"

I guess I looked persuasive because our guest paled and nodded his head. He didn't try anything as Erica removed his restraints and even went where I told him to go. He didn't balk until we approached the airlock.

"This is as far as I go," Stevens said, bracing himself against the bulkheads with his arms and legs. "Stun me if you want, but I won't just walk to my death."

I pulled an EVA harness off a hook on the wall and tossed it over Steven's arm. "If I wanted to kill you, I would have done it when I shot you. I told you that we want information. Answer our questions about Perkins' organ harvesting operation and I'll just lock you in one of the ship's cabins."

"I already told you I'm not going to answer your questions, woman."

I sighed, handed the gun to Erica, and put on my own EVA harness. "Then you'd better put on that harness."

"No."

Erica lifted the gun and gave me a questioning look. I gave a reluctant nod. My partner pulled the trigger and Stevens dropped to the deck yet again.

"Help me get him into the harness," I said as I propped the man against one of the bulkheads.

We wrestled him into the harness and then shoved him into the airlock. I left Erica guarding the semi-conscious man and went in search of a couple of things. A minute later, I tied Stevens' hands and feet, then snapped the hook from an EVA safety line around the rope tying his hands together. Finally, I put a comm into his ear.

"What about those messenger drones?" Erica asked.

Nodding, I leaned close and whispered instructions to her. Erica grinned and nodded.

"Have you got everything under control here, Nancy?"

"Yep. You run along and play with your drones."

Fingering the grimy dress she still wore, Erica said, "I think I'll put on something more practical, first. Holler if you need help."

I got into the airlock with Stevens and clipped the man's safety line to a ring just inside the hatch. I clipped my own safety line to a ring on the other side of the hatch. Finally, I ordered the med unit to bring Stevens around again. Since Erica only gave him a light stun, he came around much more quickly this time.

"Med unit, record general health information from the patient until further notice."

The unit chirped acknowledgment and I reached for the airlock controls.

"If you think staring out into space will scare me, you've got another think coming, woman," Stevens snarled.

"You should be so lucky," I said.

Air whistled around us as it was sucked from the airlock. Stevens gave me an uncomprehending look, and then the airlock hatch slid aside. Gray fog tendrils drifted into the airlock as I grabbed Stevens' arm.

Leaning close enough that our atmosphere shields overlapped, I asked, "Have you ever seen the inside of a wormhole?"

The man had time to draw in a breath—whether to respond or scream, I don't know—before I shoved him out of the airlock and let go.

As Stevens drifted away from me and the safety of the *Darkheart*, his head whipped back and forth in panic. His feet pulled at the bonds holding them together. His hands twisted around and around, trying to work themselves free from their own bonds.

If only the man knew that his life depended on the cord tying his hands together, he might not have done that last bit. I spent a few seconds contemplating the horror good old Chad would feel if he *did* work his hands free, only to discover his only lifeline to the ship was clipped to the bonds he had just cast off. Surprisingly, that vision was less enjoyable than I'd thought it would be. Besides, I still needed the man—or at least the information in the man's head—so I gave the lifeline a gentle tug.

Stevens' body stiffened in surprise when I stopped his slow drift into...whatever makes up the inside of a wormhole. The head whipping slowed and then stopped. Finally, the man's whole body just sort of slumped in relief. 'Slump' is probably the wrong word, since it seems to me that you need gravity to slump properly, but this is my personal internal monologue and I'll use whatever words I decide are appropriate. So, like I said—without saying it since it *is* internal—Stevens slumped. In zero gee.

I realized I must really be on edge. I haven't had this kind of discussion with myself since my first few hours on the *Ark 2*. At least, I wasn't actually talking out loud. Yet. Just like the events of three years ago, at least I knew why I was sort of talking to myself. Then, it was a combination of relief at my survival and confusion at my surroundings. This time, it was entirely about my surroundings. More accurately, it was *Stevens'* surroundings, since he was the one drifting outside of the ship. But I was still staring into the wormhole's mists, waiting for the whispered voices to return.

Mentioning the voices, I wondered how long I had before Stevens heard them for the first time. As soon as I thought about that, the man's body stiffened and he began looking all around himself again. What little I could see of his face had a wild expression on it as his eyes tried to find whoever or whatever was whispering gibberish to him over the comm I'd so thoughtfully provided for him.

I took just as much pleasure watching Stevens react to the voices as I did watching him panic while he drifted away from the ship. None. The man at the end of my tether could tell me where to find those missing school kids. He could, with but a few words, save the lives of hundreds of people—thousands of people if you counted future victims. By refusing to talk, he was putting his own greed and desires above the lives of countless people. By refusing to talk, good old Chad was willing to do to hundreds of families what Arktu did to me when he flushed my one true love out into the void of space. By refusing to talk, Stevens *earned* what was happening to him at this very moment.

And I *still* couldn't just kick back and enjoy the show. Maybe that's the true difference between good and evil—we good guys can do evil if we feel we have no other choice, but we can never enjoy it or even be indifferent to it.

Geez, there I go with the internal monologue again. Maybe I should just leave the philosophy to philosophers and get back to pulling information out of my captive.

The voices had been...chatting...with Stevens for about a minute now. Deciding that was a good start, I reeled the man back into the airlock. His arms were slick with sweat and his face was a rictus of fear. I pushed him into a corner of the airlock and closed the hatch. Stevens shivered as cool air rushed into the vacuum. I guess the sensation of moving air convinced him that he was safe again, because his face relaxed, leaving him looking haunted rather than terrified. The man slumped—this time properly aided by gravity—against the wall in obvious relief.

I waited until the airlock finished cycling and then said, "So, about that organ harvesting operation—where can I find it? What kind of defenses does it have? What—"

"You're wasting your time," Stevens said. His denial wasn't as vehement as it had been before I shoved the man out of the ship, but there was plenty of what my drill sergeant in boot camp called 'piss and vinegar' left in the man's tone. "You're not going to get anything from me."

"Uh huh." I leaned against the bulkhead nonchalantly and shook my head in mock pity. "You say that now. But what will you say after ten minutes outside of the ship?"

Stevens glared at me defiantly. "Your threat—which I know you'll enjoy making good on—doesn't scare me. What's outside of this ship doesn't scare me, either."

I squatted down next to the man and checked the data from the med unit. "These readings say otherwise, Stevens. Your heart rate went up to a hundred beats per minute when I pushed you out of the airlock. You took more and shallower breaths. All classic signs of fear."

Stevens tried to spin away from me so the med unit would be pulled out of my hands. It didn't work.

"Oh, and look at what happened after about a minute! That's when you started hearing voices, Chad. Tsk, tsk. A heart rate of one-forty simply *can't* be good for you." I patted Stevens on the arm in a solicitous manner. "If you won't tell me what I want to know out of concern for the children, perhaps you'll tell me out of concern for your own well-being?"

Stevens shook his head once and then fixed his eyes on the bulkhead next to him.

I sighed and stood up. "Just look at how long that safety line is, Stevens. I can let you drift *way* out there—far enough away that you couldn't see the ship through fog even if you could turn around and look for it. Does that sound like your idea of a fun time?"

Stevens kept his eyes on the bulkhead and said nothing.

"Oh yes, in case it's slipped your mind, this is a long wormhole transit—one of the longest in human-controlled space, I believe. It's fourteen hours and thirty-six minutes if our charts are correct. But we've been making the transit for the last thirty-two minutes, so let's just call it fourteen hours." I forcibly turned the man's head to face me. "At an offhand guess, you're going to spend about thirteen and a half out of the next fourteen hours outside of the ship. I wonder if I'll remember to reel you back inside before we exit the wormhole? *That* certainly would be messy, wouldn't it?"

Stevens jerked his head free of my grip and returned to staring at the bulkhead.

"Have it your way," I said.

Grabbing one of the handholds built into the airlock's bulkheads, I hit the emergency release button. The hatch slid quickly aside and air rushed out of the airlock, carrying Stevens with it.

And then everything around me vanished and I was back aboard the *Ark 2*. Wind whistled past me as the damned AI tried to flush us all out into space. Only Sko—the man of my dreams, the love of my life—was there to keep me safe in his strong embrace.

The wind of decompression ended far more quickly than I remembered from my last seconds with Sko. I opened eyes I hadn't realized I had closed and was almost surprised to find myself in the airlock of the *Darkheart*. I thanked God when the whispering voices returned, driving thoughts of Sko from my mind.

I left Stevens outside for ten minutes the second time. The next time, it was twenty minutes. Then thirty. I'll give the man this, he held out far longer than I expected, but there's only so much of that anyone can take.

Ten hours later, Stevens told us everything.

# CHAPTER SEVEN

"Where is the organ harvesting plant?" I asked.

Stevens lay on the deck in the *Darkheart's* living area. He shook and shivered, his face almost completely drained of blood. His wide eyes darted all around him as if continuously reassuring himself that he no longer drifted in the fog of the wormhole. The man gaped at me as if astounded at a voice that spoke intelligible words.

In truth, the man's hands and feet were the only parts of him that didn't move at all. Still bound with the same rope I'd clipped the safety line to, Stevens took extreme care to *not* fight his bonds. After his third trip out into the wormhole, it finally dawned on him that the cords around his wrists and ankles were as necessary to his survival as the safety line. From then on, he stopped fighting to free his limbs when I dragged him back to the airlock and closed the hatch.

My first hint that the man was cracking under the strain came when he asked me to check the knots holding his wrists and ankles together. When I refused, he told me how he was certain he felt his bonds slipping and sliding around his wrists the last time he was "out there." He almost cried at my uncaring shrug. The next time I dragged him into the airlock, he *did* cry when I refused to look at the knots. Before long, he was begging me. Each and every time, I refused while also carefully examining the bindings before pushing him back out of the airlock.

Erica watched most of this through the window in the inner hatch. She never interfered with my questioning of Stevens, but she always tried to talk me into letting her take over once Stevens was back outside of the ship. I always refused, insisting Stevens would crack faster if he faced the same implacable interrogator during his brief moments inside the airlock.

In truth, I didn't want Erica feeling what I felt every time I pushed the man back into the wormhole. I didn't want her watching her self-image as one of the good guys dissolve with each passing minute. Because, no matter how hard I tried to convince myself that Stevens deserved everything he was getting, that *he* had the power to end his torment by simply answering my questions, I knew there was more than a tinge of evil in my actions. Even with the lives of hundreds of children hanging in the balance, I knew that people throughout the galaxy would condemn me as barely any better than the man I was torturing.

And I knew those trillions of people would be right. So I lied to Erica and protected her soul.

All of this flashed through my mind as I waited for Stevens to answer my first question. Watching the man's mouth open and close, I felt disgusted with him and myself.

"Do I have to drag you into the airlock again, Chad?" I snarled. "Do you want to spend another hour out there?"

Stevens shook his head violently and fought to find his voice. "No! I- I said I'd tell you everything. Oh God, *please* don't put me out there again!"

I tried glaring at the man and found my eyes were already diamond hard and ice cold. "Then tell me where the plant is."

"Osnade."

My eyes rolled. "It's a big planet, Stevens. You're going to need to do better than that."

"An island. It's on a tropical island!"

I squatted down and leaned toward Stevens. He shrank back from me as I asked, "Does this island have a name?"

"Ploss. It's owned by the organization."

"Now we're getting somewhere," I said. "Maybe we won't have to push you out of the airlock again, after all."

The look of relief on Steven's face was so comical, I found myself laughing at him. Then I couldn't stop laughing. I laughed so hard I could barely breathe. I laughed so hard I collapsed onto a nearby sofa, holding my hands over my mouth. I laughed so hard, tears flowed from my eyes. I laughed and laughed and never realized I was really sobbing until Erica wrapped her arms around me.

Stroking my head and rocking slightly, she whispered, "It's okay, Nancy. Let it out."

I buried my face against her neck and wailed, the damage I'd done to myself finally overcoming me. Eventually, I ran out of tears and wails. My partner kept holding me, kept rocking me, and kept whispering soothingly to me.

Tightening my arms around Erica briefly, I said, "I'm okay now."

Not letting go, she asked, "Are you sure?"

"Yeah. Thank you."

"You know I'm here if you need another cry, Nancy."

"I know."

"Good." Erica stood up but kept her eyes on me. "What you need is a long, hot shower. I'll finish questioning our friend over there."

I almost protested, but one look at the determination in my partner's face stopped me. I nodded and gave her a wry smile. "You do remember we're on a spaceship? 'Long' and 'hot' aren't words used to describe shipboard showers."

"Just override the water and energy restrictions and both words will apply. Consider that an order, Nancy."

Standing, I gave Erica a mock salute. "Yes, ma'am."

In the shower, I scrubbed myself until my skin was red and I still felt dirty. Finally, I just stood under the spray and let it wash over me. Slowly, ever so slowly, the hot water loosened taut muscles. The flowing water eroded my rock-hard shoulders and untied the knots in my gut. I didn't turn off the shower and re-engage the water and energy restrictions until I felt at least vaguely human again.

By the time I returned to the living area, Stevens was manacled to the table again. He no longer shivered, but his eyes were still wide and his face pale. The man watched me walk by but didn't say a word.

I found Erica in the pilot's compartment, performing a standard wormhole exit systems check. Her eyes darted my way as I slid into my seat.

"All of the *Darkheart's* systems are operating to specifications, Captain," she said briskly. Her voice softened and she asked, "How are *you* feeling, Nancy?"

"I may not be back to specifications, Erica, but my systems are operating within tolerance."

Erica laughed, which is more than my sad little attempt at humor deserved, and appeared genuinely happy with my response. Perhaps the simple fact that I even *tried* making a joke was enough for her.

"I'm glad to hear it, ma'am," she replied. "We've got about fifteen minutes before wormhole exit."

"About?" I growled.

"Make that fourteen minutes and twenty seconds to wormhole exit," Erica responded, sounding all the world like a rebuked ensign.

We busied ourselves with normal ship's routines until the *Darkheart* shot back into normal space. I checked the nav board and was unsurprised to find a shortest-time course to the Osnade wormhole waiting for me. By force of habit, I gave Erica's energy calculations a mental double-check. They appeared accurate, which is exactly what I expected.

"We'll be cutting it close with our reaction mass, Erica," I said. "What if we need to make a run from the Osnade system after rescuing the kids?"

"Then we're screwed, Nancy. Fortunately for us, Osnade is large enough to have a Federation embassy on the planet. We'll have plenty of mass to get there from Ploss."

"I guess that will have to do," I replied. "Can I assume you got everything you needed from Stevens?"

"I got everything he knows, which isn't quite the same thing," Erica replied. "But I think we've got more than enough information to formulate a good rescue plan."

"Do you still think we should send the messenger drones?"

"God, yes, Nancy! Better to ask for help we don't end up needing than the other way around."

"Good point. Can I assume you updated the message with the information you got from Stevens?" Erica gave me such a pained expression, I almost gave a real laugh. "My apologies for doubting you, Special Agent Hampton. Please launch the drones."

Erica's fingers played over her console and a metallic thunk sounded through the hull. It was followed by a second one. Two engines lit up our scanners as the drones headed off in different directions.

"What's the transit time for the drone going to the Tokra system?" I asked.

"From this side of the wormhole, it should take thirteen hours and change," Erica replied. "It'll take the one headed for Federation space just under two days."

I checked our transit time to Osnade, comparing it to the transit times from Tokra and the nearest Federation naval base. "If Jake doesn't waste any time thinking about our request, we *might* get his help before we act. Even operating under full military thrust, I don't see how the Navy can get a ship there in time to help us."

"Maybe not," Erica said, "but I'll bet they'll come in handy when we're ready to leave the Federation Embassy."

I nodded in agreement. "Okay, fill me in on everything you learned from Stevens. We'll reach Osnade in two and a half days. I want to launch our rescue as soon after that as possible."

The first half of the trip back to Osnade flew by as Erica and I formulated and rejected and reformulated a dozen different plans to infiltrate the organ harvesting operation. Getting in was always the easiest part of the plan. It wasn't that we knew everything we would face—the number of unknowns in the operation was staggering—but at least we knew exactly *who* would face those unknowns.

Ancient Terran history never was a strong point of mine, but I know some pre-spaceflight general supposedly said, "No plan survives contact with the enemy." What went unsaid was the reason experienced leaders didn't end up as quivering mounds of anxiety. No, you can't plan for everything. Hell, you won't ever know everything you should be planning for. But if the people carrying out your plan are well-trained and keep their heads when the carefully constructed plan falls apart, you can count on them to remember their goals and make decisions based on achieving it.

In other words, I knew how Erica would respond in an emergency and she knew the same about me. We could count on each other to keep our heads and always, *always* work toward freeing the kids and shutting down Perkins and her operation. And we would have to depend on each other even more once we added a couple of hundred scared and anxious teenagers to the mix.

Approaching the wormhole exit to Osnade, we went over the bones of our plan for the fifth time.

"The plant's cover as a fish processing plant will provide our excuse to land at the facility," Erica said. "We'll use our forged shipping contract to land at their private cargo ship landing field. According to Stevens, the plant has enough traffic that we won't stand out too much."

"What do you do if the landing field's people don't let us into their landing pattern until they can confirm the contract?" I asked.

"I'll find a way to talk them into letting us land while they sort it out. Assuming most of the people who work at the plant are just normal employees, a good sob story ought to get us the necessary permissions," she said. "The next part is up to you."

The two of us spent a full day debating this next step of our plan. Like any good undercover officer, Erica pushed for a quiet and careful infiltration of the facility. We'd bypass alarms, sneak around guards, use the secret entrance to the underground organ harvesting plant, and then find the kids. After that, the whole operation would get pretty noisy, since there's no way we could 'sneak' hundreds of people out of the plant. That's why I pushed for the noisy approach from the beginning.

We argued a lot over that. I won.

"This is where our carefully formulated plan," my partner snorted when I said that, "goes off the rails. Or, more to the point, it goes off of FBI rails and onto Navy rails. We go in fast and hard, blasting anything that looks remotely like a threat. I smash through the plant's roof and land where we think we'll find the way down to the illegal part of the operation."

Erica shook her head as I finished describing the last part of our plan, such as it was. "I'm still not sure about this idea."

I waved a finger at her. "Nuh uh. We fought, I won. There's no backing out now."

"I know," she said, "but this isn't even a *plan*. It feels more like a smash-and-grab jewelry heist than a rescue."

"Because that's exactly what it is." I gave Erica a hard look. "We've been over this a dozen times. We both agree the plant's security will be built around stopping infiltrators—and there's a reason for that."

"Because Perkins and her friends are worried about spies and thieves, the kind of people who would sneak into the facility." Erica repeated my arguments almost word-for-word, she'd heard them so many times. "If we hit them fast and hard, we'll throw off all of their response patterns and bypass their security in a most unexpected manner."

"Exactly," I beamed at my partner. "Never underestimate the value of surprise. If we're really lucky, we can have the kids on the way to the *Darkheart* before anyone at the plant knows what's happening."

"But what if we get to Osnade and find Tokran help waiting for us? Or, even better, the Navy?"

"If Tokra's security people are there, we bring them up to speed on the plan and enlist their help. It would be really good if we had more than two people herding the kids back to the ship," I replied. "If it's the Navy, we let them lead the attack. Then we get to simply give the children a ride to the Terran Embassy. But we both know it would take a miracle for the Navy to be there. The messenger drone only reached the nearest navy base a few hours ago."

A little later, we exited the wormhole and got our first look at the Osnade system in nearly a week. You can imagine my surprise and excitement when our scanners detected a Federation destroyer in orbit around Osnade!

Erica and I exchanged excited glances when the destroyer appeared on the screen. Grinning broadly, I pulled up the ship's name.

"Can you set up a tight beam, scrambled connection to that ship, Erica? It's the *TFS Griffin*," I said. "Ask for a private conversation with the captain and the marine commander. Tell them—"

"I'll establish the connection with them, but I think it would be better if a decorated naval captain did the talking," she said. "I'm including your reactivation orders and your assignment to the FBI in the initial transmission."

Five minutes later, Erica and the *Griffin's* communications officer had a secure connection between our two ships. The destroyer's captain looked at me from the comm screen. He wore a commander's insignia and looked on the young side to me. But the man's eyes held the same confidence you find in good officers all over the galaxy. The marine commander, a man close to my own age, hovered in the background.

"Captain Mercer," I began, following naval custom in my address to him, "you and the *Griffin* are a sight for sore eyes. May I ask how you got here so quickly?"

Several seconds passed while my message crossed the gulf between us, followed by several more seconds as his reply did the same. "It's an honor to meet you, Captain Martin. If you were expecting to meet a navy ship here, I'm afraid the *Griffin* isn't it. We're returning from a pirate hunting mission out on the frontier and stopped at Osnade to give the crew some much-needed shore leave."

That was not welcome news. The *Griffin* must be running with a skeleton crew who were, no doubt, anxious to rotate off duty and get planet-side, themselves. Mercer could recall his crew, but I had no idea how long that would take. The *Darkheart* would make orbit in three hours and there was no way we could spare time waiting while the crew returned.

I had to assume Stevens' people back on Ruvis already sent a messenger drone on its way to Perkins or whoever their contact was on Osnade. Once Perkins knew we had her 'salesman,' she would cut her losses and destroy all evidence of her crimes. That would include killing everyone her team hadn't yet cut up for parts.

With all of that in mind, I sent a copy of the school photo to the *Griffin* and said, "Captain Mercer, I was assigned to the FBI to help find these missing children. There have been several disappearances prior to this one. In all cases, those taken were young and fit. The bastards behind this are even daring enough that they grabbed a platoon of army recruits on an overnight hike."

I waited for my words to reach Mercer and his as-yet-unnamed marine commander. Both of their faces screwed up in disgust.

"Slavers," Mercer all but spat the word. "I understand your haste, Captain Martin, but I don't know what you want the *Griffin* for. Slavery is illegal on Osnade. We'd require official orders from a flag officer before we could go after the slavers with you."

"I know that, Captain, but please believe me when I say I dearly wish my partner and I were after mere slavers. The FBI leapt to the same conclusion you did and discounted my partner's theory that there was an entirely different reason behind the disappearances. Unfortunately, her analysis is the correct one." I drew a deep breath and said, "We now know this is an organ harvesting operation. Furthermore, if our information is correct the harvesting plant is on a tropical island on Osnade."

As I outlined what we knew and our plan, such as it was, the faces of the two *Griffin* officers went through a series of expressions—from shock to revulsion to pale fury. The marine commander's face stopped there, but Mercer's face ended with thoughtful resignation.

"You said 'if your information is correct,' Captain Martin. Unless you misspoke, may I assume that means you don't have hard evidence that this...this...obscene operation really is on Osnade?"

I nodded wearily, "You may, though we have the utmost confidence in its veracity."

"I have no doubt of that, Captain Martin," Mercer said, "but I cannot mount what can only be called an invasion of a sovereign planet based on anything less than solid evidence. I'm truly sorry."

Behind Mercer, the marine commander's brows drew down. "Sir, I must protest! Let me take an assault shuttle down to the planet, gather my marines, and—"

"Major Conley, I cannot authorize that action. To ensure there is absolutely no room for misinterpretation of my words, I order you *not* to mount a mission to help Captain Martin. I do see some value in performing a readiness exercise, though. It's been a while since we performed one and I doubt the Osnade government would object to us running one now." Mercer turned his attention back to me. "I'll make arrangements with the local authorities to run this drill. By the time you make your move on the island, Major Conley should have an assault shuttle full of marines somewhere near the island of Ploss. If you discover any Federation citizens being held against their will, contact the *Griffin* and we'll send them in."

I'd have preferred having the marines from the beginning, but I also couldn't blame Mercer for his caution. In truth, I'd probably have done the same thing if our situations were reversed.

I smiled and said, "That's more than I could have hoped for, Captain Mercer. Thank you. Major Conley, tell your marines the drinks are on me if we pull this off."

Conley snapped off a salute, "That I will, ma'am. And rest assured my boys and girls know their job and are very good at it."

Though I was sitting, I returned the major's salute. "I've never known a marine who was anything but good at his job, Major."

The marine grinned and cupped a hand behind his ear. "I must be losing my hearing. I could have sworn I just heard a naval officer compliment the marines—and I *know* that never happens."

I grinned in return. "Interference from cosmic rays, no doubt."

"One more question, Captain?" Mercer asked. "I can understand why you're not contacting the Osnade authorities with this. If Stevens has connections within the Ruvis government, it's reasonable to assume this Perkins woman has them within the Osnade government. But why not contact the Federation embassy? Perhaps they could get permission for our marines to join in your operation."

"While I don't suspect any members of the embassy staff are working for Perkins, I'd rather not take the chance," I said. "And, in all honesty, I'm afraid the ambassador might order us to wait while he tries negotiating with the Osnadians. That would almost certainly take many hours. That's time I just don't think those children have."

"Understood, Captain Martin," Mercer said. "We will follow your lead in this respect.

We signed off so Mercer and Conley could get working on their 'drill.' Three hours later, we entered orbit around Osnade.

"Are you ready to talk the people at the fish processing plant into letting us land?" I asked Erica.

"There's only one way to find out," she replied.

She prepared our forged contract for transmission and keyed in the code for the plant's landing field.

Erica spoke as soon as she had a connection to the fish plant's landing field. "This is the cargo ship *Colconny* calling Ich-, um, Ichthyol-, uh..."

A man's booming laugh sounded from the comm, "Just call us Fish Field, lady. That's what all the regulars do."

Erica winked at me and her tone of voice turned just the slightest bit sultry. "Thank you, Fish Field Control. I've been puzzling over that word ever since we entered orbit. Who the hell chose a field name most people can't even pronounce?"

"This island was first settled by a bunch of fish biologists and they named the field after their field of study. I guess it's supposed to be some kind of pun on the two meanings of 'field,' but it sure makes life hard on first-time visitors."

"You said a mouthful, Fish Field Control," Erica replied. Her voice lost the bantering tone, "I'm transmitting our cargo contract, licenses, and IDs now."

The man's voice took on the same tone as Erica's, "We're receiving them now. Please switch your comm to visual so I can verify you and the pilot match the images on the licenses."

Erica's fingers danced over the controls and the face of a moderately handsome man in his mid-thirties filled the comm screen. His eyes flicked back and forth between my partner, me, and another screen on his end.

Waving his hand at the other screen, the man said, "Typical license images—they always look like crap. You're both much better looking in real life."

I almost lost it when Erica batted her eyes and placed a hand to her breast. "Why, Fish Field Control, are you flirting with little ol' me?"

Control's eyes followed Erica's hand, though I was sure the man had already noticed her display of cleavage. His eyes hadn't ignored me—I was wearing my traditional skin-tight flight suit, after all—but a perfectly outlined breast can't compete with a plunging neckline and the mysteries hidden to either side of it.

"My name is Roger," Fish Field Control said. "Feel free to use that instead of the long title."

"Thank you, Roger. I'm Erica and she's Nancy."

Something on Roger's end beeped and he frowned at another display. "Erica, I'm not getting a database match on your contract."

"What? How can that be?"

"It's probably just a data error, Erica," Roger replied. "We get stuff like this every now and then. Usually, it's because some idiot on the contracting firm's side of things forgot to file the contract or filed it too late to get here before the cargo ship."

"How long does it take to sort out this kind of thing, Roger?"

"It depends on the problem. If we have to send a messenger drone to..." Roger looked at the contract, "Tokra, it could take several days."

"That's just great!" Somehow, Erica flounced while staying seated. That, in turn, caused her breasts to heave dramatically and—based on Roger's reaction—enticingly. "What are we supposed to do while we wait for you to clear this up?"

"I'm afraid you'll have to land at one of the public fields," Roger said. "Only ships with valid contracts are allowed to land at Fish Field."

My partner slumped in her seat and raised a hand to massage her temple. "But a public field requires payment upfront."

"Sure, but all you have to do is file an expense report with your employer and they'll reimburse you. It's a pain in the ass, but—"

"You don't understand, Roger," Erica's lower lip quivered just a bit. "We don't have that kind of cash on hand and our credit is already stretched to the limit. This contract was supposed to be our big break, our chance to start digging our way out of debt."

"I'm really sorry, Erica," Roger said.

"And do you have any idea how long some companies can drag out reimbursement of expenses? Even if we had the money to pay for a private spot, it might take months for them to pay us back!" A single tear dropped onto Erica's cheek. "We had to have them write a refueling credit into the contract so you would refuel us at Fish Field. Otherwise, we wouldn't even have enough reaction mass to get back to Tokra with the cargo."

"It's against the rules," Roger said. "My hands are tied."

In the blink of an eye, distraught Erica was gone, replaced by sultry, sexy Erica. She leaned toward the vid pickup, giving Roger a much better look at the mysteries hidden by her shirt. Her mouth turned up in a teasing smile as her tongue slowly licked her lips.

"What if *my* hands were tied instead, Roger?"

The man's already wide eyes opened even more. "Um, what do you mean, Erica?"

"You heard me, Roger." Erica leaned back in her seat. Crossing her wrists as if they were tied, she lifted her arms straight up over her head. At the same time, she pulled her shoulders back, making her breasts even more obvious than before. "Just imagine silk cords tying my hands to something. Like maybe a bedpost."

Little beads of sweat popped out on Roger's forehead and he licked his lips nervously. "I...I don't know. If I broke the rules, it could be worth my job."

"Then we'd better make sure your reward is worth the risk." Erica leaned toward me and wrapped her arms around my neck. Pulling me toward her, she whispered, "Make this good. Remember, it's for the children."

I closed my eyes and tried imagining the arms around me belonged to Sko. But Erica's arms were too soft and too small. She smelled nothing like masculine sweat. Her lips were too soft, too full, and too womanly. Despite my best intentions, I found myself pulling away from Erica. Knowing that reaction could doom our rescue plans, I tried something else.

The picture of the school children formed in my mind. I saw laughing teenagers, their faces lit with excitement at the thought of their trip. Then I forced myself to imagine their fear when Perkin's people captured them. I let their fear morph into terror when they learned of their eventual fate. Certain those children were imprisoned beneath the fish factory, I knew Erica and I were their only hope for survival.

I poured all of that emotion into my return kiss. It wasn't fun nor was it exciting for me—when it comes to sex, I'm only interested in men—but it was necessary. I forced little moans from my lips and made my hands roam over Erica's face. When we broke the kiss, I pulled away slowly as if I regretted having to do so.

We both put on seductive smiles and turned to face the vid screen. Poor old Roger was just staring at us, his mouth hanging open and his eyes filled with lust.

"What do you say, big guy?" Erica purred. "Two for the price of one and the price isn't even coming out of your pocket. Grant us landing privileges and we're all yours. You can't turn that down, can you, Roger?"

The man's head was nodding long before Erica finished speaking. "Yes! I say, yes!"

"Yes *what*, honey?" my partner whispered.

"Yes, you have permission to land at Fish Field."

We both smiled broadly and Erica said, "You'll never know just how grateful we are, Roger, but we'll show you as soon as possible."

Roger grinned in return. "I get off in an hour and twenty minutes."

"No, Roger, your work shift ends in an hour and twenty minutes," Erica said, licking her lips. "You get off after you join us on our ship."

Roger gave a manic little laugh and breathed, "Oh yeah, baby!"

My partner sat back and her face returned to normal. "I'm turning off the vid now so we can both concentrate on helping my partner land the ship. See you soon."

We both fluttered our fingers in a goodbye wave. Roger was doing the same when Erica switched off the vid. We both took a moment to shudder.

My partner very carefully muted the comm and then said, "You're a wonderful woman, Nancy, but let's never, ever kiss each other like that again!"

"You'll get no argument from me," I said. "What I want to know is what happened to the woman who didn't want to dangle sex in front of Stevens back on Ruvis?"

"She saw just how effective it was at getting what she wanted from Stevens—even if only for a while," Erica said. "Never let it be said an FBI agent can't learn some new tricks, even if they come from a mere navy pilot."

We looked at each other and shuddered a second time. With an embarrassed laugh, I found the landing beacon for Fish Field and began my descent.

Descending into Osnade's tropical atmosphere, I found powerful high-altitude winds. They were much stronger than those I'd dealt with in my previous landing on the planet a little over a week ago. Even as the winds blew the *Darkheart*— or the *Colconny* as we were calling her now—off of our direct course down, part of my mind reeled at how little time had passed since we connected with Perkins and her organization.

The comm crackled to life and Roger, his voice showing no sign of the lust it contained a minute ago, said, "*Colconny*, you're drifting off course and will land on top of the factory if you stay on your current trajectory. Please follow the landing beacon exactly."

Roger's little admonishment sparked an idea. "Erica, unmute the comm and let me talk to Roger."

She flipped a switch and said, "You're on."

"Fish Field Control, this is *Colconny*," I said. "Since there aren't any other ships around us, I'm saving fuel by not fighting these strong winds. I'll correct my course when we get lower."

"I'm sorry, *Colconny*, but rules specifically state—"

"What's one more rule at this point, Roger?" Erica purred into the comm. "Besides, I already told you how close we're cutting it on fuel. If our employers screw us and we end up having to pay for our own refueling, every gram of reaction mass we can save will help."

"Look, I understand your situation, Erica," Roger said, "but this is an important safety rule. I don't want anyone getting hurt if you land on the factory."

"Isn't it entirely robotic?" she asked.

"I meant you and Nancy," Roger replied.

"Aw, that's so *sweet*, honey bunch! We'll make sure to show a little extra appreciation to you for that." Erica put a little pleading into her voice. "But you know we won't risk damaging our ship, so can't you show a little leniency?"

"I've *already* shown you more than a little leniency, *Colconny*," Roger said, striving for a more businesslike tone of voice.

"And you're getting a pretty sizable reward for that, Roger," Erica's tone matched Roger's. Then she went coy again, "Of course if you want to pay for our refueling, we could show you some *serious* appreciation for your generosity."

"Don't be stupid, *Colconny*," Roger snorted. "It would take me a year's pay to do that. Now get back on course or I'll be forced to revoke your landing permission!"

Erica glanced my way, an eyebrow arching. I checked our position relative to the factory and gave her a nod.

"There's no need to get snippy, Fish Field Control," Erica said. "We're returning to the course now. I assume you'll accept a gentle course correction?"

"Of course, *Colconny*," Roger replied. "I'm a reasonable man."

I fired the maneuvering thrusters and slowly headed back toward the beacon.

"How's this, Fish Field Control?" I asked in my brusque-pilot voice.

"Looking good, *Colconny*," Roger replied. "Maintain that course and everything should be fine."

I motioned for Erica to mute the comm again. After she did, I asked, "Can you target communications and sensor arrays without deploying the *Darkheart's* weapons?"

"I'm way ahead of you, Nancy," my partner replied, her fingers tapping on her console. "I'm programming the firing solution, now."

"Good," I said. "After you take out their eyes, ears, and mouth, I want you—"

"Do I tell you how to pilot the ship, Nancy?" Erica asked. Without waiting for a reply, she said, "No, I do not. So kindly do not tell the trained weapon's officer how to select targets."

I couldn't argue with her logic, so asked, "Would you share your attack plan with the pilot?"

"I suppose so," she replied. "The security vehicles are my secondary targets. Roger's control tower and our landing location on the roof are tertiary. By then, we should be on the ground. Well, the ground *floor*, anyway. When do you want me to rain fire down upon this hapless installation?"

"When our altitude reaches four hundred meters. Are you going to warn Roger before blasting the tower?"

Erica nodded. "Yes. He seems like a fairly decent sort, as far as horny men go."

"Are there any other kinds of men, Erica?" I asked, watching our altimeter slip below one thousand meters. "And it's not like you didn't entice that reaction from him."

"True, but can you honestly imagine a woman making that deal?"

"Maybe if the woman was talking to a male version of you, she would," I said.

Erica blew a raspberry but kept her eyes on the altimeter. At six hundred meters, she unmuted the comm again.

"Roger, honey?" she said.

"Yes, *Colconny*," Roger responded, determined to keep this professional.

"I'm afraid I'm going to have to cancel our date tonight. And you're going to want to evacuate that control tower immediately."

"Wha-?"

Erica deployed the *Darkheart's* weapons. "*Now*, Roger."

Our lasers flashed. Eight sensor and communications arrays melted under the onslaught.

"Holy sh—" Roger began.

"You're running out of time, Roger," Erica sang into the comm.

The secondary targeting solution activated and six security vehicles exploded as the lasers set off their fuel. Another two were slagged, setting the grass beneath them on fire.

As the tertiary solution activated, Erica said, "I hope Roger listened to me, but there are too many other lives at stake to ignore the tower."

I gave the scanners a quick glance and said, "I've got a small form moving away from the tower at about twenty-five

KPH. Not bad for a guy who mostly works sitting down. That's got to be Roger."

Two lasers crisscrossed the tower, slicing the top half of it off and sending it crashing to the ground. At the same time, the rest of the lasers cut a pattern in the factory's roof, causing a large section to collapse.

Erica grabbed personal comms, carefully pinning one to my collar as I brought the ship to a stop over the newly cut hole in the roof. I descended through the opening as quickly as I dared, given its narrow confines. I set the *Darkheart* down as gently as possible and prayed the factory's ground floor was reinforced. It would be truly tragic if the rescue ship crashed down into the basement and crushed some of those we came to rescue. While I did that, Erica ran back to the living area to grab our equipment.

The ship settled onto the floor. Offering up a prayer, I cut the engine's downward thrust. The ship settled onto its landing gear but nothing else happened. I left the engine idling so we could take off as soon as everyone was on board. Then I entered a locking code to keep anyone but me from engaging it and ran back to join Erica.

She wore her flak vest and three guns I could see. Holding my vest out for me, she helped me into it. While I snapped the clasps, she hooked a blaster pistol to my side and slung a grenade launcher over my shoulder. Erica handed me a blaster rifle and opened the ship's airlock. Outside, I stopped just long enough to close and lock the hatch.

"According to Stephens, the way down is over there," Erica said, pointing toward a small block of offices about twenty meters away.

Ignoring the wail of alarms and the distant shouts of security personnel, my partner and I set off to find the children.

# CHAPTER EIGHT

Close as we were to the block of offices, dropping a piece of the roof onto the floor did more than just create a door for the *Darkheart*. Pieces of the roof scattered in all directions, as did machinery all around the point of impact. By itself that was more than enough to give us a less-than-smooth path to the offices, but then we added the ship's landing thrusters to the mix. They blew crap all over the place, turning a big mess into a huge one. There were no clear routes to the offices. Hell, there were barely any clear spots where you could see the floor.

Running was out of the question. The best we could hope for was a slow jog interspersed with leaps to carry us across the least stable looking piles of roof and machinery. Meanwhile, the approaching guards had mostly clear paths toward us.

We weren't more than five meters from the ship—five meters we were forced to run parallel to our destination because of a huge hunk of mangled machinery—when the first blaster bolts sizzled overhead. Erica and I looked for the source of the shots and spotted a couple of guards standing on a raised platform about fifty meters away.

"I've got this. Keep going, Nancy," my partner said.

She raised her gun and I realized Erica chose power over accuracy when selecting her readied weapon. A *whoomp*, barely audible over the alarms, sounded from her grenade launcher. Then it sounded again. Erica was already on my tail before the first grenade hit.

An explosion sounded, followed by another a second later. The pressure wave almost knocked me off my feet. It did push Erica into my back. She caught hold of me and, between the two of us, we managed to keep moving. When the smoke and dust cleared, the raised platform was gone. I don't know if it was blown apart or simply knocked over, but no one was shooting at us for the moment.

As the echoes of the explosions faded, the shouts of the guards sounded less enthusiastic and more spread out. I also thought they weren't pursuing us with quite the same vigor as before. There were still a lot of guards out there, though, and they had much better weapons than they needed if they were guarding a simple fish processing factory.

I found an opening between machines. Past it was the closest thing to a clear path in our area. In other words, the junk on the floor wasn't more than a few centimeters deep. Even better, the path was nearly five meters long and headed in the right direction. My foot slipped as I dodged toward the path but I steadied myself on the hunk of metal that, five minutes before, was busy processing fish.

As I stumbled through the opening, Erica called, "There's blood where you grabbed the machine. Are you okay?"

I risked a glance at my left hand. Sure enough, my palm had a ragged cut several centimeters long. In the adrenaline-fueled moment, I hadn't even noticed it. Of course, it started hurting the second I saw it.

"Next time I hurt myself, don't tell me," I said. "It really smarts, now."

"Oh, waah," Erica said.

I burst out laughing. "Next time I go looking for sympathy, remind me that you have none."

"You got it, Nancy," my partner replied. "Say, do those guards sound as if they're getting a little too close for comfort?"

In response, a small hail of blaster bolts crashed into machines all around us. Sparks and hot metal fragments rained all around us.

"I'm going to take that for a yes," Erica said. "Time to dissuade our heavily armed friends again."

I heard my partner pivot on the debris covering the floor. In rapid succession, she launched five grenades. From the resulting explosions, she fired them in a wide arc designed to rattle as many guards as possible.

I continued picking my way through the factory's wreckage and despaired of ever reaching the offices. We'd been on the move for a full minute and were only halfway to our destination.

"The guards in the basement are going to have plenty of time to set up a warm welcome for us," I called over my shoulder.

"The same thought crossed my mind," Erica replied. "What about the guards up here? Do you think they know what they're guarding? I hate the idea of killing them if they don't."

"Yeah, they know," I said, scrambling over a waist-high trolley of some kind. "The guards probably rotate between basement and surface duty. Even if they don't know exactly what they're guarding, they have to know it's something highly illegal."

"Even Roger?"

I gave that some careful thought. "He probably knows something isn't quite right here, but he has no reason to spend any time in the factory. If I were in Perkins' position, I wouldn't let Roger and people like him in on the big secret."

"Thanks," Erica said. "Roger was kind of nice-guy-slimy if you know what I mean, but he didn't seem like a bad guy."

Squeezing through a narrow opening, I grinned over my shoulder and asked, "You aren't planning on having that date with him after this is all over, are you? If so, count me out!"

"Ha, ha. Based on your sense of humor—all sex and no subtlety—I'd swear you were a marine."

"Hey!" I said. "That's just mean, Erica."

"I call 'em like I see 'em," she said.

Once again, blaster bolts peppered our general location. This time, we had too much machine wreckage piled up around us for Erica to get off shots with her grenade launcher. It protected us from the guards' fire and my partner could fire her launcher just fine. The shots would hit the roof instead of arching down close to the guards, though, which didn't seem useful to me. So you can imagine my surprise when my partner cranked off five more scattered shots.

Seconds later, the grenades blew up when they hit the ceiling. Shouts erupted as blast debris—some pieces of it quite large—rained down on the guards. With an affectionate pat on the butt of the launcher, Erica tossed it aside and unslung her blaster rifle.

"The grenade launchers have..." I tried to remember how many shots Erica fired, "...um, ten shots?"

"Twelve," she replied. "I fired two at that platform right after we left the ship."

"Right. I'll try to keep count when it's my turn to blow stuff up."

By this time, we were less than five meters from the offices but I couldn't find an opening we could fit through. A tiny crevice too small for a ship's cat gave me a look at the offices. An open door lay on the other side of the pile of machines blocking our way. Without giving myself a chance to think about it, I slung the grenade launcher, grabbed a protruding pipe, and began climbing.

"What are you doing, Nancy?" Erica asked. "You're leaving our cover!"

"We're three meters from an office door and I don't think we can waste any more time being cautious," I said.

Erica cursed under her breath, but it was a curse of agreement. Slinging her own weapon again, she followed me.

Either my move caught the guards by surprise or they were too rattled after pieces of the ceiling came down on top of them. Whatever the reason, I was nearly to the top of the wrecked machinery before the first blaster bolts hit nearby.

I couldn't guess when the guards would zero in on me, so tried picking up my pace. I swung my left hand over the top edge of the wrecked machine and grabbed the protrusion it touched. Another jagged edge bit into my already sliced up hand. I gasped in pain as more blood flowed, making the surface slick. Losing my grip, I found myself dangling by one hand and supported by just one foot.

Suddenly, a hand grabbed my loose foot. "I'll push. You just hurry up and get your ass out of the line of fire."

Pushing with both legs, pulling with my one anchored hand, and boosted by my partner below, I rose up until I could roll onto the top of the machinery. Two blaster bolts hit where my butt had been a second before. More bolts hit all around Erica, who struggled to follow me to the top.

"A little covering fire would be nice," she gasped as she swung herself to the right to avoid incoming fire.

From my elevated point of view, I got my best look at what we were facing. The number of guards shocked me. "There's at least two dozen men coming our way, Erica. They're too spread out for me to give you any useful covering fire. Just wait here and—"

"You've got a grenade launcher, Nancy. Use it. Empty the damn thing at them."

I unslung the launcher while asking, "Won't we need this to get through the guards in the basement?"

"We can't risk using explosives down there until we know where the kids are," Erica replied, scuttling to her left as she fought to join me at the top.

"Good point," I said.

I rose to my knees and, following Erica's example, pointed my grenade launcher up and at an angle and aimed toward the left side of the advancing guards. I pulled the trigger, swung the gun a bit to the right, and pulled the trigger again. I kept it up until the launcher stopped firing.

The guards must have been too far away to recognize that I also had a grenade launcher because they didn't start shooting at me until the first explosion sounded. Their hasty shots flew around me, but they were still at long range and firing too quickly for much accuracy.

As the last grenade detonated, I dropped the useless launcher. Bending over, I grabbed Erica with my good hand and hauled her up next to me. We wasted no time jumping down to the other side of the machine. I dug out my portable med kit as we hurried into the office ahead of us. My partner took a few seconds to peel open a Second Skin bandage and slap it on my left palm. I gritted my teeth at her rough handling of my wound but didn't make any sound.

"How are we going to hold off all those guards out there *and* take care of the ones in the basement?" I asked.

"Damned if I know," Erica said. "Maybe we can get the marines to come in a little early?"

"It's worth a try," I said. Tapping my comm to activate it, I said, "*Griffin*, this is Captain Nancy Martin. Do you copy?"

"This is *Griffin*," Captain Mercer replied. "Have you found any Federation citizens in need of help?"

"Besides my partner and me? Not yet, *Griffin*, but we have run into extremely stiff opposition," I said. "There are too many heavily armed guards down here for this to be anything but what we suspected it was. I don't see how we can get through the guards below us without getting shot to pieces by the guards on the first floor. Isn't this level of resistance sufficient to allow Federation military intervention?"

"If this was a Federation world, yes, it would be," Mercer replied. "Since it's a sovereign world, I simply cannot intervene without knowledge that innocent Federation citizens are in danger."

I sighed. "Understood, *Griffin*. At least have the marines as close to the island as possible in case we survive long enough to find some of those citizens."

The comm crackled slightly and a new voice joined the conversation. "This is Captain Rollins of the Tokra Security Force. Please be advised that we are entering atmo now and will be at your location in two minutes. Can you hold out that long?"

Mercer spoke before I could. "Captain Rollins, are you in the Wasp class gunship we have on our screens?"

"We are," Rollins reported.

"Be advised our scanners show a squadron of Osnadian interceptors launching from a base one hundred klicks east of your position."

"Acknowledged, *Griffin*, and thanks," Rollins said. "Captain Martin, can you hold out until we arrive?"

"*Can* doesn't matter, Captain Rollins," I said. "We *will* hold. What are you bringing besides the gunship?"

"My five-man squad and as much firepower as we can carry," he said. "Sorry we cut it so close, but it took Mr. Malla longer than he expected to argue the Tokran government into sending help."

"We'll be more than happy to see you again, Captain Rollins," I said. "When you see the factory, you won't have any trouble finding our point of entry. Taking the bow of our ship as true north, I suggest you blast through the roof about twenty meters north-northeast of the bow."

"Got it, Captain. We have eyes on the factory now. We're coming in very hot, so I suggest you get under the best cover available."

"Roger that," I said. Erica and I started for a door on the far side of the office, hoping for a closet. "There are at least two dozen heavily armed guards on the first level, so be careful exiting your ship."

Nancy threw open the door and we both stared at what we saw. Instead of the expected closet, we found an open-air freight elevator measuring a good thirty meters across. A framework of support beams rose to the roof, which had tracks obviously designed to allow part of the roof to retract. Repulser mechanisms were evenly spaced around the elevator. Several more standard-sized doors gave entrance from other offices. Looking at the thing, I assumed the kidnapping teams landed their ship on the roof and brought the latest victims directly down to the basement.

Each door had its own set of controls, handily labeled in galactic basic. An idea came to me and I hit the button to open the roof.

"Captain Rollins," I said into the comm, "minor change of plans if it's not too late. Watch for a section of the roof retracting. Come through there and land as soon as it opens far enough."

"I see the roof moving now, Captain Martin. Will our gunship fit through it?"

"The Wasp is, what, twenty-five meters long?" I asked.

"About that, yes."

"Then it will fit. It will also give us all the protection we need when we descend into the basement."

Erica and I retreated into the office and shut the door to the elevator. Beyond the wreckage blocking the door, we heard the guards calling to each other as they moved our way. Meanwhile, the door to the elevator shook and rattled from the backwash as the gunship descended into the building.

A head popped up above the chunk of machinery Erica and I had climbed a minute or two ago. We both snapped off shots and the head dropped out of sight. The door behind us stopped rattling, but we weren't willing to turn our backs on the approaching guards quite yet.

"Where are you, Captain Martin?" Rollins asked.

In answer, Erica opened the door, adding, "We've got a lot of pissed off guards converging on this location."

"Roger that, Agent Hampton. Three of my men will take your place and provide a very warm welcome for those guards."

We heard the heavy sound of armored feet on metal as Rollins' men left the gunship and came our way. Their bulky armor and weapons forced them to come through sideways. Once the men were arrayed between us and the guards, Erica and I ran through the door and onto the elevator platform. I punched the descent control and then followed my partner toward the gunship.

Parts of the ship's exterior glowed from the heat generated by their rapid descent through the atmosphere and the hull popped and pinged as it cooled. We dashed up the ramp and into the crowded ship. Captain Rollins and his other two men—all as heavily armored as the three in the office—met us at the top of the ramp.

"What kind of reception can we expect, Captain?" Rollins asked.

"Hot," I said. "The guards down here have had several minutes to prepare for our arrival."

"Our ship's guns can take care of anything they want to throw at us," Rollins offered.

"No!" Erica said. "We don't know how many innocent people are held down here or where they are. We can't risk using heavy weapons until we're sure we won't hit any of them."

"Then I suggest you ladies stand aside and let us take the brunt of their defense," Rollins replied. "We're more fashionably dressed for this kind of party."

Erica and I did as the man suggested, waiting a tense twenty seconds as the elevator completed its descent. I honestly wish I could have seen the faces of the basement guards when the gunship came into view. Showing more discipline than I would have hoped, none of them opened fire on the heavily armored ship.

Then the elevator stopped. One of the armored men slapped a button and the ramp dropped with a clang. The three Tokran security officers charged down the ramp, heavy blaster rifles firing steadily.

"Let's find those kids and take them home," Erica cried.

"I'm right behind you," I said.

Then we joined the charge down the ramp.

Heavy weapons fire assaulted our ears and the sharp tang of ozone filled our nostrils before we left the ramp. All three of the Tokran security officers fired heavy blasters, holding the massive guns in both hands and changing aim by swiveling their bodies. Cables snaked from the guns to the power packs strapped to their backs, providing enough energy to fire the guns for at least half an hour. Since we'd either succeed or die long before then, they didn't have to worry about husbanding their power. Erica and I did.

We found ourselves in a circular room at least sixty meters across. The elevator came down in the exact center of the room, leaving fifteen meters of wide open space between us and the nearest wall. I saw four hastily constructed barricades spread evenly around the walls. There was a large, closed door behind each of them.

Something about the barricades looked familiar. I gave them a closer look and recognized hundreds of stasis chambers stacked on top of each other. The guards left small openings in the stacks so they could shoot without exposing themselves to return fire. Of course, they made that plan before they saw Rollins and his men. Our allies were much more heavily armed than our opponents expected.

"Captain Rollins," Erica called over the comm, "can the three of you concentrate your fire on one barricade instead of hosing down all four of them? If we can get through a door and find some Federation citizens, the marines will join us."

"You heard Agent Hampton, boys. Let's take down the one dead ahead of me," Rollins ordered. "Get your backs close to the ship for protection and then blast that thing to hell."

"Captain," I said, "those barricades are built from stacked stasis boxes. The only reason I can think of why they were in here with the elevator is because they're packed and ready for shipment. Just be aware that organs or body pieces could spill out when one is blown open."

"We're all combat veterans, Captain Martin," Rollins replied, "but thanks for the warning. Knowing what to expect is important in a firefight."

Erica and I backed onto the ramp again, giving the three men as much room as possible close to the ship. Blaster fire continued hammering all around us and a lot of it hit the security officers' armor. Smoke and dust swirled around them as their ablative armor slowly evaporated under the onslaught. I didn't know how long the armor could last, but I was pretty sure Rollins and his men were more worried about a lucky shot hitting one of their few unprotected points than they were about their armor taking so much damage it failed.

As soon as that thought ran through my mind, one of the men grunted and his left leg gave way. The man did...

something...to control his fall and, despite having a leg shot out from beneath him, ended up on one knee. He never once stopped firing and his aim remained remarkably accurate through it all. His reaction and concentration were impressive and obviously drilled into him by repetition. I never considered the level of training ground-pounders went through, but this man's automatic reaction to a wound gave me a new and very deep appreciation for their dedication.

The combined fire of three heavy blasters rapidly tore away at the barricade in front of us. Unfortunately, my theory about the stasis chambers proved right. Before long, human organs flew as chambers blew open. My stomach heaved at the sight, but I forced the rising bile back down and waited for the guards behind the vanishing barricade to give up or make a run for it. They chose running.

The door behind what was left of the barricade slid open and a new sound was added to the cacophony. Terrified screams and shouts came from beyond the door.

"Captain Rollins, Nancy and I need to get through that door!" Erica said.

"Yes, ma'am," Rollins replied. "Palmer, lay down covering fire. Once we're through the door, fall back onto the ramp for protection."

"Yes, sir," the wounded man said.

"Agent Hampton, Captain Martin, please lead the way so our armor can protect you from the rest of the guards."

Erica and I got in front of the two men and, at Rollins' command, we all ran for the open door. Palmer concentrated his fire on the barricade to our left and we let the gunship protect us from the barricade on its far side. That let Rollins and the other officer—I'd have to learn his name sometime—concentrate on protecting us from the guards to our right.

While my partner and I ran for the door, our two protectors ran *backward* nearly as fast as we ran forward. The two men kept a steady, accurate stream of fire pouring into the right barricade at the same time.

"Damn," I muttered. "Erica, remind me to salute the hell out of the next bunch of ground-pounders I run into."

"You and me, both," she replied.

We hopped through the remains of the barricade. Erica's foot came down on the arm of a dead guard and she fell.

"Erica?" I almost shouted. "Are you—"

"I'm fine. Keep going. I'll be right behind you."

Suddenly taking more care with my footing, I avoided organs and dead guards alike. Firing from the hip with my blaster rifle, I charged through the door and into a long corridor. Doors lined the walls to either side. The shouts and screams came from behind them. Ahead of me, the remaining guards showed no interest in turning to fight.

Keeping one eye on the retreating guards but otherwise ignoring them, I ran to the nearest door. It had a simple opening mechanism on the wall, which I slapped. The screams from the room intensified when the door opened. Inside, I saw at least a dozen teenage girls, all shrinking back against the far wall, terror etched on their faces. I could only imagine one reason for such a reaction—these girls knew what was done here and feared I had come to take one or more of them for... processing. I desperately wanted to hug and comfort these poor girls, but I just didn't have the time for such a gentle approach.

"Silence!" I shouted. Most of them stopped screaming, but none of them stopped crying. "I am Captain Nancy Martin of the Terran Federation Navy. We're here to rescue you. Are any of you citizens of the Terran Federation?"

I saw some of the girls misinterpret my question. One shouted, "I'm not, but don't leave me behind! God, please, you can't leave me!"

"I'm not leaving anyone," I said, "but I can get more soldiers in here if Federation citizens are in danger."

One of the girls stepped away from the others. "I- I'm Tracie Oliver. I'm from Draconis."

I wasted no time calling the *Griffin*. "Captain Mercer, I have a Federation citizen in danger."

"Understood, Captain Martin," Mercer replied. "The marines are already inbound. ETA forty seconds."

"If they land on the roof, they can come down a big opening right to us."

"This is Major Conley. My pilot says he can bring the shuttle down the shaft."

"There's already a Wasp-class gunship at the bottom, Major. The pilot won't have room to maneuver for a landing."

"My pilot begs to differ with you, ma'am. We'll see you in twenty seconds."

Muting the comm, I turned back to the girls. "Any second now, you'll hear an assault shuttle filled with Federation marines landing in the other room. There's a Federation destroyer in orbit watching over us, too."

Erica entered the room at the same time the whine of the shuttle's repulsers sounded outside. "I assume that sound means you found a Federation citizen?"

I pointed to Tracie while telling the girls, "This is Special Agent Hampton of the Federation Bureau of Investigation. She's the reason we found you. Now, can one of you tell me what's down the hall? A few guards ran down it and I don't want them getting away."

Tracie made a face. "*Her* office is down there."

"Perkins?" Tracie's face went blank, so I said, "Prim, proper woman who's always looking down her nose at you."

Tracie's face cleared and she nodded.

"Do any of you girls know if she's down there now?"

"Probably," Tracie said. "She was here checking on us a few minutes before all the shooting started. That's why we thought you were here to...to..."

"I know, honey," I said, already heading toward the door. "Erica, check the rest of the doors along the hallway and coordinate with the marines. I'm going after that bitch, Perkins!"

"You can't go after Perkins alone, Nancy!" my partner called. "Wait for me."

Breaking into a run, I called over my shoulder, "Stay with these kids, Erica. That's an order!"

"Who put you in charge?" she asked, still running after me.

"You did when you had me temporarily reactivated. Besides, you know taking care of these children is more important than catching Perkins."

"Dammit," Erica said as she stopped running.

"And don't send one of Captain Rollins' men after me, either!" I shouted. "You need them to help with the kids."

By now I was sprinting down the long hallway at top speed. I ran past at least a dozen doors on each side of the corridor and forced myself to ignore the shouts and calls coming from behind each of them. Much as I wanted to free those children, Erica and the rest of the armed force would take care of them. I saved all my breath for running after Perkins.

I slowed to take a turn to the right and found myself only a few meters from a set of double doors. They were still swinging back and forth from the guards' passage less than a minute before. Assuming those men would be waiting for me, I hugged the left wall and then dove to the right as I pushed through the doors.

A couple of blaster shots dug holes in the doors as I rolled out of the direct line of fire. I was in a square room perhaps ten meters in each direction. Two guards stood against the far wall, their guns tracking my way. A third guard was sprawled on the floor next to a closed door, a charred hole blown through his chest.

I stayed prone once I stopped rolling. While the two remaining guards kept firing as fast as their fingers could pull their triggers, I took an extra second to aim properly before firing at the man on the left. The man's shoulder all but disintegrated when my shot hit him.

As the wounded man fell, screaming, his partner's shots grew more frantic and even less accurate than before. Forcing myself to breathe slowly and evenly, I swung my gun to the right, aimed, and squeezed off a second shot. It caught him on the side. He screamed, too, and clutched at his wound.

"Neither of those are fatal wounds, *if* you get fast medical care," I shouted. "Surrender and you have my word you'll get it."

The second man I'd shot pushed his gun aside. "I give up. Just get a doctor down here!"

The first man kept rolling around in pain, though his screams had died down to loud whimpers. His flailing knocked his blaster rifle away from him, so I decided that was close enough. I rose to my feet, keeping my gun trained on them, and headed their way.

No longer required to keep all of my concentration on the two men, I finally had time to pay attention to my surroundings. I thought I was prepared for anything I would see down here, but the sight of observation windows into half a dozen gleaming operating theaters filled my imagination with horrific images.

I couldn't help but imagine Perkins pacing this room, watching as healthy children and young adults were reduced to nothing more than a collection of parts. I couldn't help but wonder what kind of sick person could conceive of something like this, much less carry it out. Right then, I swore I'd give

Perkins exactly one chance to surrender before blowing her away.

Suppressing a shudder at the horrors done in those operating rooms, I stopped a few meters from the wounded men. "Where's Perkins?"

"Did you call the doctors?" the man with the side wound asked.

"Not yet, and I won't until you tell me where Perkins is."

"She locked herself in her office," the man said. "She shot Frank when we tried to follow her."

"Good, we've got her trapped," I said, a grim smile spreading across my lips.

"No, you don't. She's got a way out to the landing field through there. Why the hell do you think we wanted to go with her?"

"She's getting away?" I shouted, wheeling around and running back the way I came. "Goddammit!"

"Hey, what about the doctor?" the wounded guard called.

"Don't worry, I'll send a medic," I replied, breaking through the doors.

Keying my comm, I said, "*Griffin*, this is Martin. Does your scan show any ships taking off from the landing field?"

"A squadron of Osnadian interceptors—the ones who came after Captain Rollins' gunship—are on hand. They've issued a no-fly order and look prepared to fire on anyone who ignores it."

"Thank God," I said. "Are you in contact with anyone from the Osnadian armed forces or their government?"

"You could say that, Captain Martin," Mercer said. "I have the Federation ambassador on one channel, Osnadian military space control on another channel, and someone from the Osnadian Department of Justice on a third. They are all quite displeased with you, I might add."

"Maybe I'll have spare time to care next week, Captain Mercer. Please alert all in question that the woman behind this operation is on her way to the landing field. She has a ship there and will try making a run for it."

"My communications officer is relaying that information now, Captain Martin. Perhaps they'll believe that more than they believed my explanation for ordering Federation Marines to join your assault on the factory."

"I couldn't care less what they believe right now. Once we put a few hundred kids in front of them, they won't—"

"Captain Martin, our scans show a small ship lifting off from the field!"

"I was hoping to capture the woman, myself, but as long as *someone* captures her I'll be happy."

"Then you most definitely will not be happy," Mercer said. "The interceptors are not stopping the ship."

"*What?*" I cried. "Why not?"

"It's broadcasting a Ruvis diplomatic ID and claiming immunity. The Osnadians are letting the ship go."

"Captain Mercer, can you—"

"No, Captain Martin," Mercer replied, his tone very firm. "I cannot and will not attack or detain a ship with diplomatic immunity."

I'd slowed to a walk when Mercer told me the situation above ground. Now I was running again. "Captain Mercer, ask the ambassador to get me a Federation ID with diplomatic immunity, too."

I switched my comm to our local channel. "Captain Rollins, I need your gunship!"

"Say again?" Rollins replied.

"The woman behind this is getting away using Ruvis diplomatic immunity. I need a ship so I can chase her down."

"Um, I don't know—"

"Rollins, there are half-a-dozen sparkling clean operating theaters at the end of this hallway. Take a good look at those kids you're freeing and then imagine them strapped down on a table while that woman has them cut into little pieces." I realized I was shouting at Rollins and lowered my voice. "Think about the contents of those stasis boxes, Rollins. Do you honestly think Perkins will simply stop doing this sort of thing? We *cannot* let her get away! My ship doesn't have enough reaction mass left for me to use her. That's why I need yours."

Rollins was silent for two of the longest seconds of my life, then he said, "The engine startup code is one eight sigma delta nine. I assume you can fly a Wasp?"

"Trained on them in the academy and flew one for two years before earning my bars. Major Conley, did you copy that? Am I running into a fire zone?"

"I copied and we've been on the ground for two minutes, ma'am." Conley sounded offended that it might take his marines that long to mop up a bunch of guards. "Everything is secure and the shuttle is not blocking the gunship's path out of here."

"Well done, Major." I switched back to the *Griffin's* channel. "Captain Mercer, how's it going with my diplomatic immunity?"

"Captain Martin, I am Hasin Gupta, Federation ambassador to Osnade." The man's tone was not friendly. "You have caused more than enough trouble for one day. No immunity will be granted."

"I have two things to say to that, Ambassador Gupta," I snarled as I sprinted into the round room with the gunship and the shuttle. "First, you are currently on record claiming the rescue of Federation citizens from a horrible death is 'causing trouble'. How long do you think your political career will last when parents throughout the Federation hear that?"

"Are you threatening me, Captain?" Gupta asked, his voice rising.

"You bet I am," I replied as I charged into the gunship. "Second, if you think I've caused trouble so far, wait until I have to shoot my way through the Osnadian defenses in pursuit of the woman behind this whole operation."

"You wouldn't dare!"

"Try me, Ambassador." Strapping into the pilot's seat, I gave the access code for the gunship's engines. As they came up to full power, I added, "Who do you think the Federation public will side with, Ambassador—the career politician who let Perkins get away or the hero of the *Ark 2*?"

"I'll see you run out of the navy on a rail, Captain Martin!" Gupta shouted.

"I already retired, asshole. I'm only active because of this mission." I added power to the repulsers and the gunship rose up the elevator shaft. "You've got about ten seconds to grant my immunity before more hell breaks loose."

"You'll pay for this, Martin," Gupta spat. "Give identity code Federation eight three alpha tango. I will authorize it when contacted by Osnadian space control."

The little gunship cleared the factory's roof. Whatever else I can say about Gupta, he kept his word and authorized my diplomatic immunity. Pointing the Wasp straight up, I pushed the throttle all the way forward and chased after Perkins.

# CHAPTER NINE

The Wasp shot through Osnade's atmosphere far faster than the *Darkheart* could have managed, even with its much larger engine. Unlike our cargo ship, the gunship was streamlined for atmospheric operations but also sported inertial dampeners so its crew could survive wormhole jumps. Fast, well-armed, and reasonably armored, Wasps are the most versatile ships in the Federation Navy. For those reasons, they are also very popular ships among the militaries of most sovereign planets.

Old navy pilots say you never forget the first ship you ever flew. As my reflexes adjusted to the Wasp's controls, I realized those old-timers were right. My fingers danced across the controls as if I'd last flown one of these ships yesterday instead of eight years ago.

The sky above me darkened to purple before turning completely black as I broke atmo. Clear of the planet's interference, my sensors easily picked up Perkins' ship. She was driving at maximum thrust toward the first wormhole in the course to Ruvis. I looked up the specs for her little space yacht and felt a wide grin spread across my face.

I had the bitch.

The Wasp had greater thrust and had similar mass. By the time she reached the wormhole, I would be right on her tail. I meant that quite literally, too. If my calculations were correct—and the instructors at the academy had made damned sure I knew they were—I'd be no more than fifty meters behind the little yacht when we entered the wormhole.

The ship's comm chimed and I answered, "Martin."

"This is Captain Mercer. I just wanted you to know I'd have blasted that woman out of space if there was some way I could have taken all of the heat on my own."

"I believe you, Captain," I said.

"You know how the Federation government works, though. They'd have filed charges against any member of my crew who followed my illegal orders. I just..." Mercer paused for a second. "That's something I just can't have on my conscience."

"There's no need to explain, Captain Mercer. I'd have done the same in your position."

"Thank you for understanding, Captain Martin. May I deliver a message to you from the crew?"

"Of course," I replied.

"Good hunting."

By tradition, that's the last thing a carrier captain says before launching fighters. The last time I heard it was mere hours before I found myself inside the *Ark 2*. I swallowed a sudden lump in my throat and gave the flight commander's traditional response.

"We'll tag 'em and bag 'em, sir."

Mercer signed off and I was left to contemplate my chase in silence. At least, that was the idea. Instead, the comm chimed again.

"Did you forget to tell me something, Mercer?" I asked as I answered the comm again.

"I believe the earnest young captain said everything he meant to say, Captain Martin," a woman's cool voice said.

"Well, if it isn't that mass-murderer, Perkins," I said.

"That's *Miss* Perkins to you, Captain Martin."

"Whatever you say, Perky. You don't mind if I call you Perky, do you?"

"I most certainly do," Perkins replied, "though I doubt my objections will stop you."

"That's a big ol' affirmative, Perky. I rank you and your objections considerably lower than I do pond scum."

"Was that necessary?" Perkins asked. "I have never treated you with anything but professional respect. Can you not see your way clear to treat me in the same manner?"

"What part of 'mass-murderer' did you not understand, Perky. I truly do not have the words necessary to convey the level of contempt I hold you in."

"At least have the courtesy to use proper grammar while denigrating me. You must never end a sentence with a preposition."

"That has got to be the single most surreal thing ever said to me, Perky. I'm chasing you down to ensure you pay for the murder of untold hundreds or thousands of people and you're correcting my grammar?"

"Why shouldn't I, Captain Martin? I hold diplomatic immunity from Ruvis. I will avoid extradition to the Federation and will never face their charges of kidnapping."

"Murder, you mean."

"No, I don't. I have never committed any crime within the Federation other than kidnapping."

"Fine, then you'll face murder charges on Osnade."

"Again, Captain Martin, any Osnadian extradition will be denied. Further, Osnade will not pursue the matter with much vigor. They benefit from trade with Ruvis far more than Ruvis benefits from trade with Osnade." Perkins made a dismissive sound. "This whole affair will produce a lot of noise. Politicians will strike poses meant to impress voters rather than achieve results. In the end, the furor will die down and the citizens of the galaxy will go on with their lives."

"What about the families of those you've slaughtered? Do you think they're just going to sit by quietly?"

"They are but a few thousand voices among trillions, Captain Martin. They'll have their moment in the spotlight and the citizens of the galaxy will feel outrage for their losses. Alas, outrage does not last forever. Some new distraction will come along and those families will fade from the public's sight."

"That's ridiculous!"

"No, dear, it's human nature."

"Let's say you're right and you'll never be extradited from—"

"I *am* right."

Ignoring Perkins' interruption, I continued, "-Ruvis. What's to stop me from simply blasting you and your ship into a million pieces?"

"Come now, Captain Martin, there's no way you, as a Federation 'diplomat', would be willing to create an interstellar incident by attacking me, a Ruvis diplomat, in Osnadian space!" Perkins chided. "How do you think the rest of the galaxy would respond to such a despicable act of war? Do you truly want to see Federation diplomats lose their immunity? Worse, do you want to risk another Fringer War, except this time against the combined forces of all of the rim and frontier worlds?"

Damn the woman, but she had me there. I wanted to stop Perkins, but not by putting untold millions of lives at risk.

Squelching my doubts, I tried another approach. "You raise a good point, Perky. It would be stupid to destroy you in front of witnesses. But we're minutes from entering a wormhole. Once we exit the wormhole, I can shred you with my ship's lasers and no one will be the wiser. But if you renounce your immunity and surrender to me, you have my word you'll live to stand trial."

Damn the woman if she didn't laugh at me. "Oh, Captain Martin, you are quite a persistent woman and not a bad actress, either. Your bluff might even work on most people. Unfortunately for you, I know the Wasp—like all Federation warships—records every single sensor reading and weapons discharge. Those recordings are sealed where the crew cannot get to them, as well."

"You're unusually well informed about Federation naval procedures," I growled.

"It's been many, many decades, dear, but I was drafted into the Federation navy and served a single term of enlistment."

Perkins' response baffled me. The Federation hadn't used the draft in over one hundred years and Perkins couldn't be more than ten years older than me. Could she be building up evidence for an insanity plea? If so, it wasn't a very good start. Besides, Perkins seemed extremely confident she wasn't going to face any kind of trial. Worse, I felt she might be right.

I looked out of my viewport as the wormhole opened before us. Perkins' ship was so close that the wormhole took both of our ships at the same time. As the mists inside the wormhole obscured the other ship, I felt despair well up inside of me at the thought of Perkins getting away with her crimes.

There had to be *some* way to make Perkins pay if I could only think of it!

My eyes slid across the Wasp's system readouts while my mind searched for a way to bring Perkins to justice for her crimes. The ship's sensor screens were blank. The weapons targeting system spun wildly, searching for something, anything, it could lock onto. The comm was silent, without static or even the usual background hum of a unit standing by to receive transmissions.

None of this was new to me. I'd piloted through more wormholes than I could remember and never saw or heard anything else. It all felt different this time because I wasn't content to simply relax and wait for the jump to end. But what could I do?

With a sigh, I slumped back in my chair and turned my gaze to the viewport. Swirling gray mist undulated outside. Then, for a few brief seconds, the mist cleared just enough for me to catch a glimpse of Perkins' ship. From my perspective, it was just sitting there forty or fifty meters away. So close and yet so far.

"Dammit!" I hadn't meant to say that out loud, but it felt good to vent out loud. "If only I could find a way to get Perkins without having the stupid ship record everything I do."

My brain twitched when I said that. I felt like there was something I was missing but my mind couldn't quite catch hold of it.

Scrubbing my face in frustration, I said, "God, it's like my brain is encased in the mists of its own wormhole. I can't get a read on anything!"

I froze as the words tumbled from my mouth. Pulling my hands away from my face, I stared at the controls again. They weren't reading anything. That meant they weren't recording anything, either. More accurately, the systems were recording a whole lot of nothing. I was tempted to try coaxing the weapons into targeting the other ship—a trick that's supposed to be impossible inside a wormhole—but that would give the system something to record.

If I was going to make Perkins face frontier justice, I didn't want to give away my intentions by fiddling with the weapons. So far, anyone examining the record of this chase would only have the threats I made before we entered the wormhole. If the ship's records proved I never acted on those threats...

I glanced into the mists outside of the Wasp again. Without giving myself a chance to think about what I was doing, I got up and headed for the ship's storage compartments. It only took me a few minutes to find everything I needed—safety lines, an EVA harness, and a small jetpack. Next, I checked the weapons locker and was quite impressed with the wide assortment Captain Rollins and his men brought with them. I grabbed a couple of magnetic explosives and a remote detonator.

Minutes later, I stood in the Wasp's airlock wearing the EVA harness. My blaster still sat in the holster where Erica placed it just before we left the *Darkheart* back at the fish factory. I had the explosives in a pouch clipped to my belt along with three extra safety lines. Stuffing the detonator into a pocket, I fastened one end of the fourth safety line to the ring next to the airlock's hatch and the other end to myself. Taking a deep breath, I cycled the airlock and crawled out into the mists of the wormhole.

Moving hand-over-hand, I pulled myself to the front of the Wasp. Seconds after I left the ship my comm filled with whispering voices. Like before, the whispers quickly formed short, pitiable sentences. Like before, I *think* it was my imagination. Like before, the words gnawed at me.

*"You've got to stop her, Nancy."*

"Don't worry, I will."

*"She can't get away again."*

"She won't."

*"Don't let anyone else end up like us."*

"I won't. You have my word."

*"I can't rest until she pays."*

"You'll be at peace soon."

*"You're the only one who can do it, Nancy."*

"I'm on my way to stop her now."

I hoped the voices would fall silent after I answered them. They didn't, even when I launched myself from the bow of the Wasp. I kept answering the voices as I paid out the safety line. Seconds or minutes later—I couldn't tell which—I reached the end of the first line.

I stopped responding to the voices while connecting the second line to the first, giving all of my concentration to changing the connections in the right order. I fastened the second line to the first line. Next, I snapped the other end of the second line to myself, carefully using a different safety ring on my harness. Finally, I disconnected the end of the first line from my EVA harness, taking extreme care so the end of the second line remained attached.

I heaved a sigh of relief when I finished and tried to get my bearings. The fog of the wormhole obscured both ships. Turning myself so I lined up with the safety line that stretched back to the Wasp, I triggered a short burst from the jetpack.

Once again, I spoke to the voices as the second line slipped through my fingers. Once again, the voices never stopped talking. Once again, I fell quiet while adding the third safety line, again sighing in relief when I finished. Finally, I sighted back along the line again and fired the jetpack for a few seconds. Some unknown time later, I did it all again when I added the fourth line.

I was at a complete loss for what to do when I reached the end of the fourth line without reaching Perkins' ship. My head whipped back and forth as I searched for something, anything that could show me where to go. Whatever moved the fog didn't choose that moment to give me a clear view of the ship. No shape loomed out of the mist showing me the way. All I saw was swirling tendrils of fog.

Up or down? Left or right? Those directions had no real meaning out here, but they were the only descriptions I had. Which direction should I choose? I had no idea. Refusing to be paralyzed with indecision—or, perhaps, unwilling to keep talking to the whispering voices—I decided to go down. Carefully swinging my feet up and my head down, I reached for the jetpack switch.

*"No, Nancy, not that way!"*

*"You're going the wrong way."*

*"We're over here."*

I knew I was in a vacuum, but I swear to God the voices came from up and to my right. Once again, I reoriented myself, this time pointing in the direction the voices came from. With my fingers poised to fire the jetpack, I hesitated for a few seconds. The voices pleaded for justice again so I triggered the engine.

I almost cried with relief when Perkins' ship slowly took shape in the mist. Grabbing one of the ship's external safety rings, I immediately pulled myself along the side of the ship toward the airlock. Prepared to use the pair of remote-controlled explosives to get into the ship, I sighed with relief when the hatch slid aside when I activated the airlock controls. Once the ship's artificial gravity took hold of me, I disconnected the safety line from my harness, clipped it to a ring on the ship's hull, and closed the airlock.

The second the outer hatch sealed, the inner hatch slid open. Inside, Perkins quickly backed away from the airlock controls but kept a blaster trained on me the whole time.

Perkins wore an EVA harness much like mine. The woman was obviously expecting me, which explained why I didn't have to use my explosives to get through the airlock. I guess I made more noise crawling across the hull of her ship than I thought.

"I underestimated your level of determination, Captain Martin. I don't impress easily, yet you impress me," Perkins said. She pointed at my waist with her free hand. "Using one hand, unbuckle your gun belt and drop it on the deck. My blaster is set for stun, so don't think I won't fire."

"You don't want to kill me for all the trouble I've caused, Perky?"

The woman's already cold eyes chilled a few more degrees. "I do wish you would stop these infantile name games, Captain Martin. While I admit your little nickname irritates me, it will not drive me to distraction. As for killing you, I never let personal preferences get in the way of business."

"Of course. I've got a whole body full of useful products."

"In other times, you'd be quite correct. Now, after all of the trouble you've caused...well, let's just say I have another use for your body."

"Don't leave me hanging, Perky. Do tell me what diabolical plans you have in mind for me."

A very unpleasant smile spread across Perkins' face. "I haven't had access to such a fit and attractive body as yours in many decades, Captain Martin. The red hair and blue eyes are definitely an added bonus."

A shiver ran up my spine at the woman's matter-of-fact tone and the possessive way her eyes roamed over my body. I've been ogled by men and more than a few women. I've watched them mentally undressing me. I've stood against the sheer force of their lust and, on more than one occasion, kicked their asses when they wouldn't take 'no' for an answer. None of that prepared me for the look in Perkins' eyes as she stared at me.

Trying to keep my voice level, I said, "You're not making any sense, Perky."

Shaking her head in mock disappointment, Perkins said, "You're a smart woman, Captain Martin. Your actions have made the situation too hot for poor Miss Perkins. I'm afraid I'm going to have to retire her and begin as someone new."

"Me?"

"You."

"But our body types aren't remotely similar. The best cosmetic surgeons in the galaxy couldn't—"

Perkins' laugh cut through my protest. "Dear child, I deal in *organ transplants*, not cosmetic surgery. There isn't an organ in the human body that can't be transplanted. You know that."

"Good God," I whispered, "you're going to have your brain transplanted into my body."

"And your brain will be transplanted into this body. Don't forget that." Perkins smiled widened. "I think I'll have the surgeons sever your brain's communication centers, but otherwise, I'll leave you mind intact. Just imagine yourself trapped in this body *and* inside your own mind!"

Perkins paused for a second, perhaps waiting for me to say something. I wanted to scream, but I couldn't find my voice.

Shrugging, she said, "I'll write a heartfelt confession before the brain switch and my friends in the Ruvis government will see that this body—with your damaged brain inside it—is extradited to the Federation for trial. Imagine living out your days locked inside your own mind, silently screaming as your sanity slips away. It's so delicious it sends a tingle down your spine, doesn't it?"

The horror I felt must have been evident on my face because Perkins' evil smile slid aside, replaced by her normal, businesslike expression. "But if you cooperate with me, Captain Martin, if you don't give me any trouble, I swear I will kill you quickly and painlessly after the transplant is complete. You can have the blessed relief of death's embrace instead of a century or more of mute torture. Just be reasonable, Nancy, and your suffering will end before it even begins."

I tried wrapping my mind around the horror Perkins proposed for me and simply failed. The woman nodded her head as if in sympathy.

"It's a lot to process, dear, but I promise it's in your best interests to cooperate. I've been doing this since before your great-great-grandmother was born and am quite experienced at it. You simply cannot win." She said it in a voice both maternal and terrible. "Now, show me that you want to cooperate by taking off that gun belt."

The mundane request to disarm myself snapped my mind away from contemplating this woman's evil and back to finding a way to make her pay. There had to be some way to end her and the horrors she represented. Even as my right hand moved toward the gun belt, I remembered something else I brought with me. Maybe Perkins was right and I couldn't win against her—but maybe I could salvage a tie.

With Perkins' attention riveted on the hand slowly working on the buckle, I raised my left hand a few centimeters until it brushed against the pouch containing the two magnetic explosives. Perkins' eyes never left my right hand, giving me some hope I could turn the tables on her.

With a soft clank, the end of the gun belt slipped through the buckle and the whole thing dangled from my right hand. As before, Perkins' concentration never wavered from the gun now swinging back and forth in front of my knees. I extended my right arm toward Perkins and dropped the belt. At the same time, my left hand darted to the clasp fastening the pouch to my EVA harness. I dropped my gun belt at the same time I pulled the pouch free. With a quick motion, I tossed the pouch backward.

Perkins must have caught my throw in her peripheral vision because her head snapped up and her eyes locked on my left hand. At the same moment, I heard the extremely satisfying clunk of the magnets attaching themselves to the outer airlock hatch.

"What was that?" Perkins demanded.

For the first time since the inner airlock slid open, the woman directed her attention at something other than me. I took advantage of her lapse and dove to the right. A hasty blaster shot scorched the air where I'd just been. My left leg tingled as the bolt brushed against it in passing. Meanwhile, my right hand dug into a pocket and pulled out the remote detonator.

I rolled away from another shot while flipping up the protective cover on the remote. I pressed and held the single button. Two cheerful chirps sounded from the airlock hatch. Rolling up onto one knee, I held the detonator in front of me.

"Shoot me and it will be the last mistake you ever make!" I said.

Perkins trained her blaster on me but didn't shoot. "What is that in your hand?"

"This? Just a remote detonator for the two magnetic explosives attached to the outer airlock." I turned the unit so she could see the button I kept pressed. "If I release this button the explosives go off."

I got to my feet and walked toward Perkins. "If that happens, the last thing you'll hear is the swoosh of explosive decompression, before you're swept out into the wormhole to die a long, lingering death as your oxygen runs out."

It was Perkins' turn to stare at me in horror. I reveled in it.

"What's the matter, Perky? Nothing clever to say?"

"You won't do it. I know you won't, Captain Martin."

"You sound like you're trying to convince yourself more than me, Perky."

"No, I'm just pointing out the obvious. If you release that button, you'll die, too."

"Gosh, Perky, I never thought of that. Let me carefully consider my options...I can surrender to you and die. Or I can kill you and die. Either way I die, but one way, you die, too." I scratched my head with my free hand. "That sure is a tricky decision. Yep, it's quite a conundrum."

Perkins held both hands in front of her as if trying to calm me down. "Okay, I see your point, Captain Martin. I tell you what, I'm going to put down this blaster, okay? Then *you'll* be the one in charge and no one will have to die."

Keeping her finger off of the blaster trigger and carefully pointing the gun away from me, Perkins slowly crouched and put the gun on the floor. She lifted her hand away from the gun and looked up at me.

"Stand up slowly and kick the gun over to me, Perky."

"*Stop calling me that!*" she screamed.

Perkins launched herself at me from the crouch, catching me completely by surprise. Her hands wrapped around my right hand, forcing me to keep pressing the detonator button. Perkins' feet churned, driving me back against the nearest bulkhead.

Once again, my navy training took over. I slammed my left fist into the side of Perkins' head while jerking my right hand down in an attempt to break free of the woman's two-fisted grip. Perkins' head rocked to the side from my blow, but she recovered quickly and head-butted me in the nose. Pain blossomed and blood flowed, but I was past caring about such mundane things.

I felt Perkins' fingers digging at my grip on the detonator, trying to pry it from my grasp while still keeping the button pressed. Deciding I wasn't going to beat Perkins into submission anytime soon, I grabbed her throat with my left hand and squeezed. She tried drawing a breath and barely managed a pathetic wheeze. Her face turned red from the exertion and lack of oxygen. If anything, that made her more desperate than before.

While still prying at my fingers, Perkins slammed our hands against the bulkhead. My grip loosened just a bit, so Perkins pulled our hands back to do it again. As she did, I tried spinning her around so I could slam her head into the same bulkhead.

My hand smashed against the metal and it opened involuntarily. Perkins, with one finger still on the button, had the detonator. Then her head crashed into the same hard metal. Dazed, her hand spasmed and the detonator fell free.

The two little explosives blew the airlock's outer hatch away. In the massive decompression, Perkins and I were swept toward the void.

The wind pushed us toward the yawning hole that was all that remained of the outer hatch. We caromed off a bulkhead, our rush toward the void slowing briefly. Everyday shipboard items—from tools to cups to data pads—bounced off of us before continuing their headlong rush to oblivion. Hands grabbed my EVA harness and climbed toward my head, bringing a shrieking voice with them.

"*No, I can't die!*" the voice wailed. "*Not like this! Not after I've been through so much!*"

Ignoring the irritating voice, I searched for a different one. A gentle voice. A laughing voice. A courageous voice. A loving voice.

"I'm coming Sko," I heard myself say. "We'll finally be together again."

"*Don't give up, you stupid bitch!*" the irritating voice screamed. "*You've got to save us!*"

I thought I heard the barest whisper from the loving voice. I hadn't heard that voice in so long that I almost cried. But what had the voice said? I couldn't understand it over the irritating squawks of the other voice.

Absently, I punched at the source of my irritation. It whimpered in pain and fell silent. All around me, wind howled and things carried by that wind clattered off of metal walls. I ignored them and concentrated on hearing that one, longed-for voice.

"I couldn't hear you, Sko," I called. "Are you welcoming me?"

In that moment, despite my headlong rush toward the mists of the wormhole, I heard the voice clearly. Sko's voice.

"*You need to let go of me, my Captain.*"

"No, I can't! You're—"

*"Dead. I'm dead. But you, my Captain, my love, you still live."*

"But I can't keep living without you, Sko!"

*"You can, my Captain. People need you."*

"But I need you. I don't know how to go on without you."

*"You're stronger than you know, my Captain. Be strong now for those who will need you later."*

"But—"

*"It is not your time, my love. Take my hand and live!"*

At the edge of the hole, a hand caught mine. My left arm jerked as I stopped and pain blossomed from my wounded palm. I looked up, expecting to see Sko's smiling face. I saw no face. I saw no hand except my own. It clutched the airlock safety ring. In my bitter disappointment, I almost let go of the ring. Then I remembered Sko's words and tightened my grip. Part of my mind insisted the words were from my imagination. I ignored it and held on as the last of the ship's air blew past me.

My eyes tracked all of the junk blown out of the ship, before lighting on Perkins. She never lost her white-knuckled grip on my EVA harness. Her wild, wide eyes locked on mine. Then she pulled herself up and reached for a higher grip.

Without conscious thought, my free hand punched Perkins in the nose. I felt it flatten and break. I watched blood bubble from it, forming little red spheres around her face. I saw her fierce grin turn feral.

"You caught the safety ring, Captain Martin, and saved me," she said, and I heard her because the fields of our harnesses overlapped. "Even *you* want me to live!"

"Like hell I do!"

I punched her again. As her head rocked back, I pulled one leg up and worked to wedge it between us. Perkins fought every move I made, shoving down on my leg and trying to climb farther up my harness.

Punching her in the face wasn't working, so I went for the same stranglehold I used before the airlock blew. When my hand drew close, Perkins thrust her face between my thumb and index finger, and then her teeth snapped down on my hand. The pain was so intense I almost lost my grip on the safety ring, but Perkins was distracted, too.

She concentrated so hard on biting my hand that she stopped pushing down on my knee. I jerked my leg up and my knee cracked into Perkins' jaw. I yelled again as my knee forced the woman's teeth deeper into my hand, but my leg also put some needed distance between the two of us.

I drew my other leg up and worked my foot onto her breast. With her wide eyes and her face covered in blood and drool, Perkins truly looked the part of a crazed villain fighting for her life.

Slowly, inexorably, I straightened my leg. I screamed once more as Perkins' teeth tore free from my hand. Then I got my other foot onto the woman's chest. I hammered on her hands, which still gripped my harness. I pushed her away with my legs.

Perkins' grip on the harness loosened. Sensing the inevitable, she suddenly released my harness and wrapped both arms around one of my legs. Terror-struck eyes met my pitiless stare as I raised my free leg.

*"Don't do this! I'll surrender to you. I'll stand trial for you. Please, don't leave me out here!"*

Driven by rage and pain and grief and horror, my boot slammed into Perkins' face. I heard the beginnings of a terrified wail from the woman before our atmosphere fields separated. Perkins tumbled away, her screams muted by the vacuum of the wormhole. Then the mist swirled, and she was gone.

I don't know how long I hung from the safety ring, my breath coming in gasps, before I finally pulled myself back into the ship. With gravity holding me to the deck again, I headed for the pilot's console. My hands throbbed and bled, but I ignored them. Calling up charts for the system at the end of the wormhole, I plotted a course and instructed the autopilot to follow it when the ship returned to normal space.

Once that was done, I returned to my safety line. Despite the explosion and the fight at the airlock, the line was still where I left it. Working with the same care I used adding safety lines during my trip to Perkins' ship, I attached the line to my harness. I pulled myself back toward my ship, never once fully releasing the line. The voices still whispered though they no longer formed words or sentences. I found them surprisingly comforting. In less time than I expected, the Wasp loomed out of the mist. Minutes later, I slumped into the pilot's seat and gave my wounded hands over to one of the ship's portable med units.

Much later, the wormhole exit alarm woke me. Shortly, the Wasp burst back into normal space. I checked my sensor screen and watched as the autopilot on Perkins' ship executed my course. The ship's engines flared to life and drove at full power toward the nearby sun.

Two hours later, a solar flare reached out and engulfed the ship. All evidence I was ever aboard went with it. Perkins was dead. Her ship was gone. The Wasp's sensor recordings couldn't incriminate me.

Numbly, I turned the Wasp around and returned to Osnade.

# CHAPTER TEN

I had one hell of a reception committee waiting for me when I emerged from the wormhole back into the Osnade system. At my best guess, half of the Osnadian Navy was on hand and more than ready to blast the Wasp into tiny pieces. Fortunately, the *TSF Griffin* was there, too. Captain Mercer kept reminding the locals that I had diplomatic immunity and that firing on me would be an act of war. Even then, Mercer suggested I dock with his ship and return to Osnade under Federation military protection. I accepted and brought the Wasp into his ship's small landing bay.

Emerging from the little ship, I saluted Mercer. "Permission to come aboard, Captain Mercer?"

Mercer returned my salute. "Permission granted, Captain Martin."

"It appears I'm quite popular around here," I said.

"You have no idea, ma'am. Ambassador Gupta ordered me to throw you in the brig."

"I'm pretty sure my return to active duty is nearing its end, Captain Mercer. Please just call me Nancy."

"Very well, Nancy. I'm James."

"Do you think I could get a couple of minutes in a shower before you lock me up, James?"

"My cabin and facilities are at your disposal. And you won't be spending any time in the brig."

"You're going to ignore an ambassador's orders?"

"In this case, yes. Besides, Gupta doesn't scare me nearly as much as your partner does." James stopped outside the door to his cabin. "She wants to talk to you quite badly. We'll arrange a tight beam comm connection with her while you're in the shower. Comm the bridge when you get out and we'll patch her through."

He keyed open the door and saluted once again. "You'll find a clean flight suit laid out on the bed. Agent Hampton assumed you'd want to change and told us your size."

As soon as the door slid shut, I peeled out of my sweat-stained and grimy flight suit and padded to the shower. I spent two and a half minutes of sheer bliss scrubbing myself clean. Pulling on the flight suit, I commed the bridge and was immediately connected to Erica.

She had concern written all over her face as she examined me through the comm screen. "Are you okay, Nancy?"

"Yeah. What about the kids?"

"We got here in time. We've verified all 216 of the kids from the school along with a couple of dozen from earlier groups." Unconsciously, Erica ran a hand through her hair. "Honestly, we saved more than I dared hope, but...Oh, God, Nancy, there are so many we didn't save!"

I nodded in understanding. "At least it's over, now."

"Is it?" Erica asked, her eyes searching my face for some hint of the answer.

"Is this a secure channel?" I asked.

"Completely. Captain Mercer isn't recording it and is leaving it out of his logs. Anything you say now will stay between us."

"Perkins is definitely dead."

"You're sure? Mercer told me her ship dived into the sun when it exited the wormhole, but how can you be sure the woman was onboard when it fried?"

"She wasn't onboard, Erica. The last I saw of Perkins, she was vanishing into the mists inside the wormhole," I said, and then gave my partner an abbreviated version of my fight with Perkins.

"How much do you think she suffered?" Erica asked when I wrapped it up.

"If she was smart enough to accept the inevitable and removed her EVA harness, not very much," I said. "But that just doesn't fit what I learned about her during that short fight. I expect she drifted for hours as her oxygen supply slowly depleted, listening to the whispering voices, and slowly losing whatever sanity she possessed."

"And what about you, Nancy? How are you doing?"

"Much better since hearing we saved all of those school kids."

"Good. I can't wait to introduce them to the woman who saved their lives."

"They've already met that woman, Erica," I said. "You did the investigating. I just came along at the end and helped attack the factory."

"You did a hell of a lot more than that! I'd never have gotten to this point on my own. Come on, Nancy, you're the hero of this case."

I shook my head. "I've been a hero, Erica, and once is enough. This one is yours—which is as it should be."

My partner's deep brown eyes searched my expression for a few seconds before she nodded. "If that's the way you want it, I'll do what you ask. But at least agree to meet with the kids. They deserve the chance to thank you."

"Assuming Ambassador Gupta doesn't turn me over to the Osnadian government to stand trial for...what? Invading a sovereign planet? Destruction of property? Anyway, if I'm still free—"

"You were instrumental in rescuing nearly two hundred and fifty Federation citizens from certain death. Privately, the Osnadian government may wish they never heard of you. Publicly, they'll smile and humbly proclaim their gratitude to you and everyone else involved in the rescue." Erica made a 'come here' motion with her hand. "So, come on down and meet the kids."

"All right, if you insist," I said. "Are you still at the factory?"

"Are you kidding? We got the kids away from there as fast as possible. We're at the Federation embassy." A voice called something from off cam. Erica nodded in response and then turned back to me. "Art—um, that's Captain Rollins—says to bring his ship back, assuming it's in one piece."

I laughed, "Tell him that I didn't even scratch the paint. I'll go see James—Captain Mercer—and get clearance for departure. Can you send him the coordinates of the embassy?"

"He already has them. See you soon, Nancy."

James escorted me back to the destroyer's small launch bay. I was surprised to see the marines' assault shuttle landing.

"We had to call them back sooner than planned. Ambassador Gupta asked the *Griffin* to take the news of the rescue back to the Federation." At my quirked eyebrow, James added, "It serves two purposes. First, it gets us away from any pesky questions Osnadian politicians might have concerning the 'exercise' that had the marines so close to the fish processing plant. Second, and a far more important, we can get the news back as quickly as a drone could while giving a human touch to the delivery."

I took a moment to salute and thank each of the marines personally, while swearing I'd make good on the drinks I owed them. Then it was time to board the Wasp and head for the embassy. Captain Mercer surprised me by giving me full honors, including piping me aboard the Wasp.

My landing at the embassy was equally formal, including the pretense of a warm welcome by Ambassador Gupta. The man was a good actor. Standing right before him, I barely detected how uncomfortable he was during the proceedings. Cheered by that, I smiled brightly and thanked him for his kind welcome. As soon as she could reasonably do so, Erica stepped in and led me away from the pomp.

My partner took me straight from the ceremony to the kids. I wish I could say our meeting was like Christmas morning and your birthday rolled into one, but it wasn't. The kids spent so long with the threat of death hanging over their heads they couldn't truly accept they were safe. The kids smiled and some even laughed, but their eyes were haunted.

No strangers to heartache and hardship, Erica and I spent the rest of the day and the entire night with the kids. We listened when they needed a sympathetic ear. We talked when they needed to hear from someone who could relate to their ordeal. And, seeing the kids' sheer terror that Perkins would return for them one day, I broke my own rule of silence and told them of our fight within the wormhole.

We stayed with the kids for three more days. When their families arrived, I faded into the background and let Erica accept the thanks. Much later, she sought me out in our shared room.

"You got your wish, Nancy. Apparently, I'm the designated hero of this story."

"You're the *real* hero, Erica. God above, please tell me you can see that?"

"I know I worked hard on this case and *do* deserve some credit, but I didn't do it all by myself," Erica said.

"Do you think I took down the AI on the *Ark 2* by myself?" I asked. "I can assure you I didn't—but I'm the only official 'hero of the *Ark 2*' according to all the stories. And you're the official hero of this case, so get used to it."

Erica didn't look happy about it but nodded her acceptance.

"Have you figured out what you're going to do now, Nancy?" At my answering shrug, she said, "You could join the FBI. The Agency could use someone like you."

I'd been expecting the offer, so already knew my answer. "I'm flattered, but I'm a pilot, not an investigator. Getting back behind the controls during this mission reminded me just how big a part of me piloting is."

"I hoped you'd choose otherwise, Nancy, but I understand."

"I don't suppose the FBI would let me keep the *Darkheart*?" I asked.

"I asked them to give the ship to you, but the Bureau said no," Erica replied. "If you want to get your butt back into a fighter, you could sign up with one of the various corporate navies."

I considered that for a few seconds. "That never occurred to me, Erica. Even an ancient starfighter is better than no starfighter at all."

"You know GenCo makes the current generation starfighter. Their pilots fly the same ship you flew in the Fringer War. Maybe you should check them out."

"Maybe I will." I hugged my soon-to-be-ex-partner. "It's been good working with you, Erica. Look me up if you ever end up in the same system. I'll do the same."

"I'm going to miss you, Nancy."

"Same here, partner."

I never liked protracted goodbyes. At the FBI's request, I agreed to pilot the *Darkheart* back to their shipyard. With nothing else keeping me on Osnade, I filed my flight plan the next morning. While Erica was busy with the kids and their families, I slipped away from the embassy. By the time she returned to the Federation, I was long gone.

* * *

I fired all of my maneuvering thrusters, spinning my fighter to starboard and putting it into a tight roll at the same time. Laser shots flashed through my old location as the remaining enemy ship missed its shot. Gunning my engines, I brought my ship around the large freighter that was the real target for that last enemy and his now-vanquished buddies. Skimming the big ship's hull, I caught the last ship making a cautious orbit of the freighter. With the target's bulk masking my fighter, the lone bogey didn't see me until I fired on him.

"You're dead, Tom. Return to base," the comm crackled. "Nice flying, Captain Martin. Please return to base, also."

"Roger that, GenCo Control," I said, falling in behind Tom and the other three starfighters in the 'bogey' force.

My comm buzzed, indicating a private channel. "Martin."

"That was some impressive flying out there, Captain." It was Tom, my last victim.

"Thank you, sir," I responded.

"I was a lieutenant when I retired, ma'am. I can safely say I am in no way your superior."

I laughed, "GenCo Human Resources is going to consider your opinion of me when deciding whether to hire me or not. You remain 'sir' until they make that decision."

"Captain Martin, you could call me 'asshole' and I'd still tell HR to offer you the job before some other company scoops you up."

"Thank you, sir," I said, then we both switched off the private comm and gave all of our concentration to landing.

I was the last to set down and had both the fighter maintenance crew and the four 'bogey' pilots waiting for me as I climbed down from the cockpit. The maintenance crew began checking the fighter for damage even before my feet touched the deck.

The crew chief met me, data pad in hand. In a bored voice, he asked, "Anything to report, ma'am?"

"Yes, your ship isn't properly tuned." The chief's head lifted in surprise as if he wasn't expecting a mere job applicant to offer any criticism. I continued, "The starboard engine is producing about two percent less thrust than it should. At a guess, its reaction mass feed isn't rich enough. Conversely, the reverse thrusters feed is too rich, causing them to hesitate for a fraction of a second when I took them from zero to one hundred percent thrust."

The crew chief just kept staring at me, making no entries in his data pad. Back in my navy days, I'd rip a new one in any crew chief who did that. Could I do that now and still hope to land the job? If I couldn't, I decided GenCo wasn't the kind of company I wanted to work for.

"Did you get that, chief?" My voice echoed off the landing bay walls as I brought out my pissed-off-flight-commander voice. The man's eyes widened in surprise at my tone, adding to my irritation. "In a real fight against a swarm of real enemies who are really trying to kill the pilot of this craft, those issues could spell the difference between life and death. When you and your team screw up this badly, you only pay with a bad mark on your record. The pilot pays with his life."

I got up into the face of the crew chief, who took a step back in alarm. Poking the man in the chest to emphasize every word, I said, "So when I tell you about a problem, you write down everything I have to say and then you and your team check out the ship and keep checking it until the problem is fixed. *Do you understand*?"

"Yes, ma'am!" the crew chief said. Then he started tapping on his data pad, muttering enough of it to show he was entering my comments.

I turned back to the pilots and found them all struggling to hold in laughter. They gave up once I looked at them.

"She got you, Chief," Tom said around his laughter. "And the look on your face was priceless."

"Would someone let me in on the joke?" I asked.

"Chief Stanley always sets up some little issues with the fighter used to test applicants," Tom said. "He says pilots don't know crap about the ships they fly and this is his way of proving it. You just showed him how wrong he is."

"Captain Martin showed me I was wrong about *her*," Chief Stanley said. "That doesn't let the rest of you flyboys off the hook."

I spun back around to face Chief Stanley, my face red with anger again. "You send pilots out in ships you *know* aren't one hundred percent ready to fly?"

"It's never anything major, Captain Martin," the chief said, holding his hands up in a placating manner. "Your ship was a fraction of a percent off, nothing more."

"Tell me something, Chief." I pointed across the landing bay to a hoist supporting a starfighter engine while several technicians worked under it. "What would you call a pilot who fiddled with the hoist's brake so it was 'a fraction of a percent off' while you were working under it?"

The man's face paled. "That would be...irresponsible."

I nodded, "Damned right it would. And that means what you've been doing with this starfighter is...?"

"Irresponsible."

"Exactly." I whirled at a muffled laugh from behind me. Glaring at the four pilots, I added, "What I truly can't believe is that fellow pilots knew about this stupidity and didn't do anything to stop it. If you were under my command, none of you would be laughing right now."

Leaving all five men staring at me, I stalked to the locker. Fifteen minutes later, showered and dressed in my own clothes, I was still cursing the five men. I had, no doubt, ruined my chance of getting the job and decided to just follow my usual routine of slipping away unnoticed. Only that didn't work this time.

"Captain Martin?" A woman I recognized as a member of HR waited for me outside of the locker room.

"I can find my own way out, thanks," I growled.

Her eyebrows rose in surprise. "Are you no longer interested in the job?"

"After the scene in the docking bay, I thought GenCo might no longer be interested in me."

Comprehension dawned on the woman. "Rest assured, that is not the case. I'll admit the base commander is angry, but not at you."

A few minutes later, the woman ushered me into an office. A woman I hadn't met sat behind a large desk. She motioned to a chair without taking her eyes from her data pad. She kept reading for another minute or so before looking up.

"In all my years with GenCo, I don't believe I've ever met a more qualified applicant for a job than you." She glanced at the data pad. "Captain Quincy had nothing but praise for your time on the *Phoenix*. Everyone associated with the *Ark 2* project speaks highly of you. Special Agent Hampton of the FBI says the only possible reason for not hiring you is because an idiot is in charge of GenCo HR. Our four test pilots and the crew chief concur. Indeed, they claim the tongue lashing you gave them is further proof we should hire you."

"That is...gratifying to hear," I said.

"No doubt," the woman said. "While I like to think I'm not an idiot, I do have one concern I wish put to rest."

"You're afraid I'm an alcoholic," I said.

"You do come right to the point, don't you?" A ghost of a smile played across the woman's face. "Yes, that is my concern. Considering your words after the test flight, I am certain you can see the problems inherent in putting a drunk in a state-of-the-art starfighter."

"I can, and wouldn't have accepted a job offer from GenCo if you hadn't brought up this subject." I paused to give the woman a chance to say something. When she remained silent, I continued, "The FBI turned on the alcohol scrubber in my implant for my recent assignment with them. I asked them to leave it on when I left. Furthermore, I am willing to have the navy give GenCo the access code to my implant so they can verify the scrubber remains active."

"That, Captain Martin, is exactly what I wanted to hear." A real smile appeared on the woman's face. She tapped on her data pad before presenting it to me. "Is this offer acceptable?"

I scanned the details and fought hard to keep my eyes from popping out of their sockets when I saw the salary. It was three times what I made flying for the navy. I pressed the 'accept' button, let the pad take a retina scan, and handed it back.

"Welcome to GenCo, Captain Martin," the woman said, offering me her hand."

"Thank you, ma'am," I said. "May I ask where I'll be stationed?"

"We have a real need for someone of your skills at GenCo's busiest space station. Among GenCo employees, I'm afraid it's known as the armpit of the galaxy. But it also draws more than its share of illegal activity, including a fair bit of piracy."

"It sounds well suited for me, ma'am," I responded. "What's the place called?"

"Pegasus Station."

"That's a lovely name, ma'am."

"Trust me, it's not a lovely place."

I flashed a humorless smile. "Perfect."

If you enjoyed this book, please post a review on Amazon.com. Reader recommendations are the best advertising.

# ABOUT THE AUTHOR

Growing up, Henry worked at the usual range of menial jobs — from grocery store bag boy to pizza delivery to retail sales — before ending up in software development. In between the menial jobs and the IT jobs, he achieved some small fame as the writer and co-creator of the small press comic book titles Southern Knights and X-Thieves. For the past ten years, Henry has also taken up the mantle of professional storyteller, performs regularly throughout the state of North Carolina, and has recently released his first book of children's stories.

Henry has been a fan of science fiction for as long as he can remember. He has loved space opera and planetary romance since the beginning, that is why his science fiction novels end up in those subgenres.

Henry currently live in Raleigh, NC, with his wife, son, two cats, and lots of imaginary friends all clamoring to tell him of their adventures.

www.ingramcontent.com/pod-product-compliance
Lightning Source LLC
Chambersburg PA
CBHW020958180626
46814CB00003B/1145